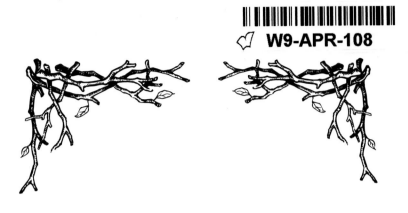

DEADWOOD

Kell Andrews

SPENCER HILL
MIDDLE GRADE

Spencer Hill Middle Grade: An Imprint of Spencer Hill Press

Please visit our website at:
www.spencerhillmiddlegrade.com

Second Edition: June 2014.

Andrews, Kell, 1969--

Deadwood : a novel / by Kell Andrews - 2nd ed.
p. cm.
Summary: A twelve-year-old boy gets a message from a tree telling him it's cursed — and so is he.

The author acknowledges the copyrighted or trademarked status and trademark owners of the following wordmarks mentioned in this fiction: Barbie, Boy Scouts, Bran Buds, Cirque du Soleil, Dr. Evil, Game of Life, Gone with the Wind, Good Housekeeping, Google, Heisman, Hostess, iPod, Jedi, Junior Mint, Kiwanis, Lexus, Lions Club, Lucite, Nestle's, Ouija, Philadelphia Eagles, Tasmanian Devil, The Answer, U2, Van Halen, Walmart, Wikipedia, Ziploc.

Cover design by Shawna Tenney
Interior layout by Jennifer Carson and Marie Romero

ISBN 978-1-939392-07-7 paperback
ISBN 978-1-939392-71-8 ebook

Printed in the United States of America

To Jeff, Juliette, and Oona

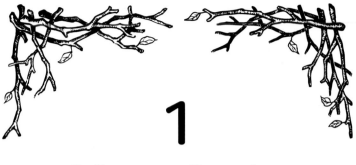

1

A Ranger Running

Martin Cruz knew something was wrong the moment he saw Lower Brynwood from the interstate. The town center was nothing but a few crummy blocks that slanted downhill, looking like they might slide off in the next hard rain.

Turned out there never was a good, hard rain. Storms blew by as quickly as possible, watering the lawns of Upper Brynwood at the top of the hill and leaving Lower Brynwood nothing but gray skies and dirty water foaming in the creek. Mud flows downhill, as Martin's mom liked to say. Except sometimes she didn't say mud.

Martin picked up the pace of his run and settled into the steady rhythm of heel strikes and deep breaths. He turned into the park entrance, reveling in the crunch of the first fallen leaves beneath his feet. When his mom was home, they would rake huge piles to jump in, but they never got around to bagging before the wind scattered them again. Aunt Michelle wouldn't tolerate a leaf out of place on her own lawn, and a glimpse of an unraked lawn anywhere in Lower Brynwood triggered a little twitch in her temple that signaled her irritation.

To take his mind off being forced to live in his aunt's perfect house, Martin replayed a game of *Dragon Era* in his mind, trying to remember each challenge. When he came here, he'd thought he'd be able to keep playing online with Gord and Zach, but Aunt Michelle wouldn't let him play at all, much less subscribe to the massive, multiplayer online version of *Dragon Era*. He was stuck imagining the game.

Imaginary or not, it was still better than being in this miserable town. Instead Martin was a powerful rogue ranger trekking the Marlician Forest. He was fleet-footed and eagle-eyed. The very trees shielded him, and he feared no man or beast.

Martin chugged now, his legs burning as he climbed the final big hill. He wasn't used to these inclines—there were no hills like this near his mom's Army base in South Carolina—but he felt his spindly legs getting stronger every day.

He turned a corner on the hard-packed path, heading for that big old tree with the carved bark he always touched before he turned back. The tree was tall and ancient, the bark silver-gray like antique metal, the crude carvings as incomprehensible as runes. It seemed to be more than a tree. He felt as if it waited for him—an ally, a kindred soul in the forest primeval. It might have been damaged and abandoned, but still, it grew. Just like Martin.

But today the tree was not alone. It was under siege.

A circle of red and black jackets surrounded the trunk. What were those kids doing here? Great, a bunch of jocks—probably from the high school. Martin slowed up. He hated that kind of kid—mostly because they hated him first.

A tall blond guy said something Martin couldn't hear. He smirked at his own joke like he was hosting a talk show, and everyone else laughed along. Then a bigger guy with wide shoulders and a square head stepped up. He brandished a short knife in his hand and drew attention by feinting as if he was in a choreographed knife fight. The blond leader laughed again, clapping. Everyone joined in, their hands in rhythm.

Martin thought of the brutal rituals of the mercenary clans in *Dragon Era*. He observed like a ranger would, and planned his attack. Who knew what kind of bloody initiation he had stumbled into? What were these cretins going to do to each other?

Then the big guy shrieked a war cry and chiseled violently at a smooth spot in the tree's bark.

Martin flinched as if the knife had pierced his own flesh. That was his tree.

Blood throbbed in his ears, louder than the clapping. His mom always said that when you get angry, you make mistakes. But he also knew to deal with any hostile in the forest quickly, without mercy. And these jocks were hostiles.

After just a few weeks, he thought of this as his trail. His woods. This scarred-up beech was the closest thing he had to a friend here, and he wasn't going to let anyone damage it again. If he had to escape, he could. They might be jocks, but Martin could run fast, and he could run far. And he didn't have a varsity jacket weighing him down, either.

He stepped into the fray.

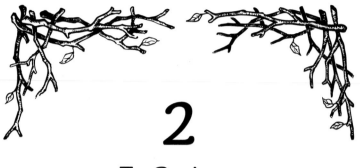

2

To Be Low

Hannah Vaughan had lived in Lower Brynwood her whole life, and yet even she knew something was wrong there. Flowers grew feebly, if at all. Freshly painted trim on the old brick homes peeled as soon as it was dry. The only birds that managed to survive were starlings and crows.

The town was even nicknamed Lo-B, which reminded Hannah that everyone in town had settled into a lower state of existence. *To be low. I am low. She is low. They are low. We all be low.*

Lower Brynwood hadn't always been this way. Hannah's parents talked about a time when the high-school football team went undefeated, and everyone who graduated had a job waiting for them at the steel mill or the Happy Elf Bakery. Now the factories sat shuttered, and the few shops that remained on Main Street were nail salons and check-cashing stores. All the good luck had run out, as if the town was a horseshoe somebody had nailed upside-down.

Tonight, before the home opener, the football players and pep squad would dedicate their season at the Spirit Tree, the oldest tree at the highest spot in Lower Brynwood.

Legend held that the ancient beech had been a lookout in the Revolutionary War. This outpost had been important then—the mill had supplied the Continental Army in Valley Forge, and Thomas Brynwood had been a hero, running reports on British troop movement to General Washington, along with the gunpowder shipments.

That was ancient history. For as long as Hannah could remember, the seniors at Lower Brynwood had carved their class year into the silvery bark to make their own mark before the home opener began. And every year, they lost that game, homecoming, and most of the games in between.

But this year, things were going to change. If her brother Nick led the Lower Brynwood football team to victory, he would be the first one in their family to go to college. And if he did that, Hannah knew she would follow him.

But first the Lower Brynwood Black Squirrels had to win.

"It doesn't matter either way," Hannah told her brother at breakfast Friday morning before the opener. "A doorknob can see how talented you are."

Nick gulped down his orange juice and wiped his mouth with the back of his hand. "Doorknobs don't scout for college teams. It doesn't matter how many passing yards I rack up. Coaches want to see me win. And I need all the luck I can get."

"You say you make your own luck."

"Then I need to make some fast. No scholarships for losers."

The hall phone rang. Hannah ran to check the caller I.D.—Waverly Wiggins. Waverly was supposed to be at the Vaughan house already.

Hannah picked up the receiver. "Don't say it—I can guess."

"I'm sorry, Hannah. I'm way behind in math, and my dad's making me study," Waverly said.

"I'll help you catch up tomorrow at school. Just don't cancel."

"I already suggested that, but Dad doesn't trust me. Mr. Michaelson told him I talk too much in study hall when I'm supposed to be working."

"Well, you kind of do," said Hannah. When she sat with Waverly, neither of them ever did half as much homework as they planned.

"If you feel that way, go without me." It was obvious Waverly thought Hannah was as likely to go to Mars.

"Fine. I will." Hannah hung up without another word. She could handle going alone.

She pulled her dark-blonde hair into a ponytail, dragged her bike up the stairs through the basement hatch doors, and pedaled toward the scrubby patch of woods called Brynwood Park.

The ceremony had already started when she arrived. Nick flashed a grin at her, but she didn't know how to break into the circle of jostling, over-loud high-school kids. Without Waverly next to her, she didn't want to. Instead she lingered at the edge of the group, wondering why she had come at all. She was just a seventh-grader—they didn't need her here.

Hannah was mapping out an escape when she noticed a very skinny, sweaty boy stalking out of the woods. She couldn't quite make out what was happening inside the circle of red and black jackets, but this boy seemed to know exactly what was going on, and she was pretty sure whatever he did about it would be a mistake.

Hannah had seen him before. He was the new kid at school, and not many new kids showed up in Lower

Brynwood. She'd meant to say hi, but he'd had his iPod plugged in his ears at the time, so she didn't bother. Now he tore the white earbuds out and strode toward the circle. He was going to start a fight, Hannah realized. No way.

"Drop the knife." No one seemed to hear the command, reedy and shrill. The boy spoke again, this time roughening his voice into a growl. "Step away from the tree and drop the knife."

The wall of red and black jackets convulsed, a few dozen faces turning. For a split second the football team must have expected a cop, because they looked relieved to see the red-faced boy with wild, curly hair.

"Who are you?" asked the guy with the knife. It was Chase Roberts, Nick's friend.

"Martin Cruz," the boy said. He threw his shoulders back and glared. "That's my tree. And nobody's going to be cutting it."

Chase snorted. "Your tree? I hate to break it to you, but this is the Lower Brynwood Spirit Tree. We've been carving it for good luck since before you were born."

"How's that good-luck thing working out for you?" Martin said, his voice squeaking again. "You couldn't beat Upper Brynwood with a stick."

"You little creep." Chase stepped forward, but Nick stopped him with an outstretched hand.

"Leave him alone. I'll take care of this," he said to his teammates, and they turned back to the carving. Nick put one hand on Martin's shoulder, steering him away from the ceremony and toward Hannah standing at the edge of the circle. The skinny kid twisted in Nick's grip, his face screwed up.

"What are you going to do? Beat me up?" he asked.

"What are you, eight? I don't beat up little kids," Nick said.

"I'm twelve."

"I'll put it this way—I don't beat up anybody if I can help it." He let go, and Martin shrugged him off, stumbling back. Nick turned toward his sister. "Hannah, you know this kid?"

When Nick spoke her name, the smaller boy seemed to notice her for the first time. She was so tall she probably looked like she belonged with the rest of them, even if she didn't.

"He's new. In a couple of my classes, I think," she said, tracing the dirt with her toe.

"Okay, Martin. Maybe you don't know much about Lower Brynwood, but this is a tradition."

"It's a stupid tradition," Martin grumbled. "A stupid town. You keep hacking at that poor tree for luck, but it never brings you any."

"Maybe. But I need a little luck right now. We're the underdogs, Martin—not the bad guys."

"I can't let you do it," Martin said, his voice firm but quiet. A cheer went up from the group, and the football players stepped away from the tree, admiring their handiwork.

"Hey, take a look, Vaughan!" Chase called. "Lo-B rules!"

Martin grimaced. "Rulz with a Z. Fool wrote Lo-B Rulz."

"Sorry, kid. It's done," Nick said. He sighed, and Hannah couldn't tell if he was sorry to have missed the carving or sorry that it had been done at all. "Hannah, I'm getting out of here. Do you need a ride?"

She shook her head. "I've got my bike."

"Fine. But get home quick—those storm clouds are rolling in fast. And Martin—welcome to Lower Brynwood."

Nick followed his friends as they crashed down the hill, straight through the brush to the gravel parking lot beyond the tree line. Hooting and shouting, they seemed to have forgotten about Martin. Hannah couldn't help thinking that was a good thing. He looked crushed already, and Chase hadn't laid a finger on him.

Hannah walked over to the tree and traced the fresh carving with her fingers. "Poor old thing."

The letters were damp, like a bleeding, badly spelled tattoo. The older carvings circled the tree, stretching to a height seven feet off the ground. Gaps had formed in some letters, the cuts fading into the bark's ridges until they were barely legible, while others looked as thick and sore as scar tissue in skin.

Not *like scars*, Hannah realized. They were scars. The beech was alive—it wasn't some old rock or sign to be painted and repainted each year. And it wasn't as if the tradition actually brought them luck. Maybe Martin was right.

She looked at the boy, who shook with mute fury, glaring in the direction Nick and his friends had gone. He wiped tears from his eyes with the palm of his hand and turned toward the tree. "So, why don't you get out of here? You're one of them."

"Not really," she said. "I'm one of me."

"Just get out of here. It's going to rain any minute."

"It'll blow over. It always does."

The wind gusted, and the sky boiled and tumbled, rough as seas. Hannah heard the raindrops on the leaves before she felt them—a drumming, and then a deluge. She pulled her bike in closer to the tree trunk and leaned against the scratchy bark. Her fuchsia-colored bike had been a birthday present—the first girl's bike she had ever owned after twelve years of dented hand-me-downs—and she wasn't going to let a few drops of rain ruin it. She'd wait.

She threw her head back and studied the canopy a hundred feet above, where masses of ridged green leaves churned and swayed in a pattern that defied geometry. She felt dizzy.

The rain thickened, like a spigot had been turned on. This time the storm arrived for real.

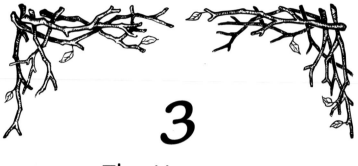

3

The Message

Martin didn't want Hannah there. He said in his most Jedi-like voice, "It's not safe to stay. Under a tree is the worst place to be in a lightning storm." Every Marlician ranger knew this, even if Martin had actually learned it in Boy Scouts.

Hannah rolled her eyes. "It's just rain."

Then a bolt of lightning hit the tree with an explosion louder than anything Martin had ever heard. He slammed his body to the ground, arms over his head, though he knew he couldn't protect himself from a lightning strike. The force overwhelmed his senses. He felt the power flowing through the tree's trunk, saw with magnified clarity the loose strands of Hannah's fair hair standing out straight from her head in a halo. She sprawled motionless after diving away from the tree, yet Martin could feel her vibrating with energy, a buzz coming off her skin as surely as if he was touching her.

Yellow-white brightness surrounded them, and then it was gone. The world went slack and gray as the electricity faded. Even the rain stopped.

Martin's eyes watered and his ears rang. He felt his arms and legs, sore where he had thrown himself to the ground, but he was intact. Hannah hadn't moved yet. "Are you okay?" Martin asked.

She nodded, her hair drifting back into place as she stood. "That was a close one." Her eyes, already wide, opened further, showing all the whites around her irises. She gasped and said, "Closer than we thought. Look behind you!"

Something glimmered in Martin's peripheral vision. He turned around, and the glow brightened. The electricity hadn't gone.

The tree was on fire. The bark swelled and crackled, light escaping from fissures in the surface, like liquid lava beneath the blackened surface of a volcanic flow. Martin jumped back, wary—that wasn't how wood ought to burn. The glow strengthened, and Martin realized the streaks of light weren't random cracks. They were letters and numbers. The messages carved in the bark were written in fire.

2001 gets it done. '95 alive. Party like it's 1999. 2006 4ever. LBHS rocks 1992. Lo-B Rulz.

"Get away. The tree is burning from the inside," Hannah said, her hands trembling. She looked hypnotized, like she couldn't take her eyes off the tree.

"It's not burning." This was no fire—at least, no fire he had ever seen. The light glowed golden, more like the sun than flame. Like pure energy. Like magic. Martin stepped close again, his hand hovering over the bark. He didn't detect any heat coming off the surface. He touched a carving hesitantly. The bark felt cool. The light faded into black.

"I think the fire—or whatever it was—is out," he said.

But it wasn't. The light had concentrated in one place, growing stronger, then fading and reappearing four feet higher in the bark, as if the flow of energy had moved beneath the surface. The light blinked out, and the glow popped up in another carving, and then another. Then it reappeared in the original place, and then the next, cycling through quicker and quicker. Letters flashed bright as neon, one at a time.

The tree was trying to tell them something.

Holy crap. *A tree was trying to tell them something.* Hannah backed off, like she wanted to bolt but was afraid to turn her back on the electrified tree.

"It's a code," Martin said. He felt as if the light was coursing up his spine into his brain, which hummed and cranked through every cipher he had ever heard of, images of numbers and letters scrolling through his head. The tree was communicating—he had to figure it out. "If it's a code I know, I can break it."

Hannah was pale and jumpy, but she still managed to correct him. "It's not a code. It's a word." She shook her head so hard her brain must have slammed against her skull. "A tree is spelling a word. No way."

The carved H in LBHS lit up, then an E. A. L. "Heal," Martin said. Was Hannah right? Could it be so simple? Could a tree know English? The lights repeated, then faded out.

"The tree spelled 'heal,'" Hannah said. A new word began—an M, then an E. "Heal me."

Martin expected the message to stop, but it didn't, racing through letters faster than a Ouija board. "Heal me. End the curse. Heal all." At the last word, the tree blazed with light, as bright as the lightning bolt had been, and then the light disappeared as quickly as the lightning had.

"The tree…was talking to us," Martin said. His tree had spoken. He had understood.

"No. It was texting us." Hannah frowned, still shaking her head. "No way. That's impossible."

"You saw it."

"I don't know what I saw."

"I do," he said, gaining speed as he spoke. "I knew it wasn't just a tree. It's something more. It's a spirit. Your brother called it the Spirit Tree."

"Spirit Tree, like *school* spirit. It's not possessed by spirits," she said, hugging her arms to her chest.

"It's not possessed. It's communicating," Martin said. "No one was listening until now." He was in this town for a reason after all.

"The tree is trying to tell us it's cursed?"

"I don't think just the tree is cursed. It's the people who carved it who are cursed. Lo-B. Lower Brynwood. More like Lower Deadwood," he said, squinting at the tall blonde girl, who set her mouth into a line. Of course she wouldn't believe. He jabbed a finger toward her. "People like you."

Hannah squeezed her eyes tight. "I just got a text message from a tree. This can't be happening. I must be dreaming."

"Then I'm dreaming, too," Martin said. "And somehow we're in the middle of the same dream."

"As if you and I would ever have the same dream," she said.

"That's how we know this is real." He gritted his teeth. "Look, you saw it. You read the message out loud to me. 'Heal me. End the curse.'"

Her eyes snapped open. "Then maybe the electricity turned the tree into a cell-phone tower, picking up signals. Or maybe the lightning did something to us instead— crossed the circuits in our heads. Fried our brains. Because trees don't talk. They don't send text messages. It's not possible." She stood up.

"You're going to turn your back on this?" Martin said.

"Watch me."

"I don't need you, anyway!" Martin yelled. "I knew you were one of them." Hannah had already swung a leg over her bike. She hurtled down the hill in a spray of mud. He lost sight of her in the brush and gloom before she reached the bottom.

"I should have known she wouldn't help," he said aloud. She was gone, and he was glad. Martin put his hand on the tree. The sudden storm had darkened the woods so he could no longer see the carving—just rain-blackened bark. After being so angry earlier, he felt strangely calm. He had thought the tree was the only friend he needed, and he was right. A talking tree was no more bizarre than an elf or a dragon or any of the other creatures from *Dragon Era*. It was somehow more plausible. At least he knew trees existed. Why shouldn't a tree send messages? Why wouldn't it be cursed?

"I tried to stop them," he said. "Stupid jocks. They deserve to suffer."

The light flared up beneath the bark, and a thrill passed through Martin. He backed away for a better look—another message was coming. The letters lit up in sequence.

"*Heal me. Stop the bad one. End the curse*," Martin read. *The bad one.* He shivered. "Heal all." Then the message changed. "*End the curse. Heal yourself.*"

"Myself?" he repeated. "What did I do? I'm the one who tried to help. And I can't be cursed. I'm already stuck in Lower Deadwood. It's not like things could get any worse."

Martin suddenly thought of his mother, halfway around the world in an Afghan war zone, and realized that his life could be far, far worse. He felt cold. He was alone in the forest now, the way he had wanted it, just him and the trees, but now he wasn't sure this spirit was his friend. This was magic—real magic—but what kind? It felt dangerous. If a tree could speak, it could also lie. And who was the bad one? Was he—or she—watching him right now? This was too much, too fast. He'd been preparing for something like this his whole life, but he wasn't ready.

"That's it. I'm out of here, too." He turned for Aunt Michelle's house, but as fast as he ran through the woods, he heard a creak and crackle above his head, as if an electric charge leapt from branch to branch, following him as the trees swayed, crossing branches in the wind. Martin stumbled over rough ground, twigs snapping underfoot. He peered over his shoulder, half-expecting to see the forest collapse into a tangle of old wood, vines grasping to drag him into the rubble.

Finally he burst out of the trees and into the wide streets of Brynwood Estates, which Aunt Michelle proudly called "the most prestigious development in Lower Brynwood." Martin suspected there wasn't much competition for that title. Usually he hated the cardboard-box conformity that passed for affluence around here, but today he was so glad to see it, he almost kissed the sidewalk.

Amid the ordered houses, Martin ran past a moss-covered cottage, surrounded by brambles like Sleeping Beauty's castle, seemingly abandoned except for laundry that flapped on a clothesline stretching from the porch. Some of the sheets and underwear had blown off into yellowing briars and drying stands of perennials. A striped sheet twisted in the branches of a gnarled dogwood, torn and caught fast.

Martin knew just how it felt.

4

The Spirit Tree

The way trees remember is nothing like the way you remember.

Yet the beech recalled a time when the sky was distant and the ground close.

Those creatures that moved on two legs—humans, it learned—towered above it.

They cleared the land around it with axes and scythes and fires, but still the tree grew. Without siblings for cover it stretched toward the sun. As it outgrew the humans, they sheltered beneath it, and its branches stretched outward.

Days and seasons passed. Its roots delved downward into the earth and wider than its branches. It drew in water and minerals, which surged upward against gravity. It reached for the sun and turned light into food—first for itself, but with bounty to share. Bees and hummingbirds swarmed to its blossoms, caterpillars fed on its leaves, squirrels gorged themselves on the nuts that weighed its branches down and tumbled to earth.

It breathed, exhaling oxygen and ions that streamed upward to the heavens like prayers.

Spring passed, and summer, until each autumn when the tree shed its leaves, sealing itself tight for the cold winter. When days lengthened the tree's sap surged, its buds swelled. The tree opened, and the wind bore its scent to the animals that awoke.

Around the tree the humans crawled like ants, smaller now and distant, moving too quickly for a tree to sense clearly. They fought and bred and labored, building homes and mills. Each human was replaced by two more.

Two hundred summers or more passed. The tree couldn't quite keep track of time or the humans.

The buildings decayed, falling in their own season, just as leaves did.

When the buildings fell, the plants grew again—the wildflowers and grasses, shrubs and vines. The tree watched from above as a new forest grew around it and beneath it.

Until humans came again. They moved too quickly to sense. A bad one led them as they spoke loudly and carried something sharp.

The tree had seen grasses shorn and trees tumbled, but it hadn't felt a blade for two hundred years. The tree had been wind-torn, nibbled and bored by insects, scraped by the antlers of deer long dead. This blade was different.

For two hundred years, water had risen through the heart of the tree. Now something sucked it dry, pulling its life upward, wresting it outward through the leaves. The tree drew more water, and still the greedy thing drained it.

The knife wounds scarred over but the damage continued, ceaseless and merciless, year after year. The land around the tree burned dry. The scent the wind carried was metallic and sharp, as if poisoned. Bees and hummingbirds stayed away.

The humans did not. In their season they returned with blades in their hands. They spoke loud words, carved into the tree's surface, and laughed.

The tree did not feel pain. It felt absence. It felt what was stolen. It felt the bad one grow strong as it weakened, and all the life around it faded.

For two hundred years and dozens more, energy had streamed through the tree from the earth to the sky.

Then a girl put her hand into the carved runes and spoke the words aloud. The tree understood her. The lightning came down, a bolt from above.

The tree gathered the electricity about it. And it spoke.

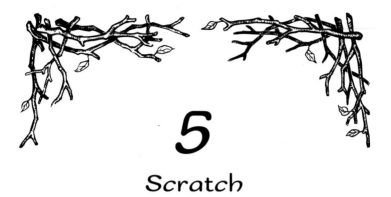

5

Scratch

Back in the dingy basement, Hannah grabbed a musty towel out of the laundry basket and dried her bike. With a brother on the football team and one who worked as a landscaper, no one would notice a little extra mud and grease. She tossed the towel into the old washing machine.

She shivered, grabbed one of Nick's fleeces out of the dryer, and stripped off her new-school-year jeans and T-shirt. They looked a lot like the clothes her best friend Waverly wore, except that Hannah had made-up, discount-store brands instead of designer labels. She didn't really care, and somehow nobody else in seventh grade cared what she wore, either. She was a Vaughan, starting forward of the Lower Brynwood Middle School soccer team and younger sister of two high-school quarterbacks—one past and one present. Being a Vaughan was a label that counted in Lo-B. That and a dollar got you a cup of coffee at the Quik Mart, Hannah's dad joked when Nick and A.J. got too full of themselves. Which was pretty often, if you asked Hannah.

She packed her wet clothes into the already-full washer, dumped in a cup of powder detergent, and started a heavy-duty cycle. She felt something soft brush against her leg, and leaned down to pick up her small gray cat.

"There you are, Vincent Vaughan Gogh." She stared into his amber eyes, daring him to start blinking in Morse code, but he was just a cat. No talking, no texting. Didn't want anything but dinner and a belly rub. Just as he should be.

She trudged up the basement stairs, kissing the silky dent on the top of the cat's head between his ears, or where his ears would have been if he had had two of them and not just one. He'd been bloody and scrawny when Hannah first found him, but his torn-off ear had healed up just fine. He was still scrawny, though, no matter how much she fed him. The cat purred, and Hannah purred back.

The kitchen bustled with noise and glare. Hannah sniffed—something spicy, something sweet.

"I was just wondering where you were," Hannah's mother said. She was still wearing mismatched scrubs from the nursing home where she worked as an aide. "Grab a bowl."

Nick and A.J. hadn't waited, digging into big portions of slow-cooked chili. Hannah set down Vincent, who leaped to the windowsill and huddled in the purple glow of the plant light shining on a tray of African violets. She filled her bowl but picked at the chili.

"Weird thing at the Spirit Tree, huh, Hannah?" Nick asked. She whipped her head up. How did he know about the messages?

"Why? What happened?" A.J. asked, then stuffed a piece of cornbread into his mouth, crumbs raining into his bowl.

"Some kid tried to stop the ceremony," said Nick. "Didn't work. Can't stop Chase once he gets going." Hannah relaxed. Nick didn't know anything.

Hannah's mother *tsked*, then said, "The poor guy had the right idea. Carving that old tree isn't my idea of a ceremony. It's vandalism."

"It's an old tradition," said Nick.

"Not that old. Nobody did it when your father played ball." She glanced at Hannah's father for confirmation, but he only mumbled, his mouth full. "That's right. Back then no one thought defacing your community was a good way to show your school spirit. Don't know why the teachers shut their eyes. Somebody ought to stop it." She looked pointedly at her husband, who shrugged. Hannah's father worked at the township planning commission, and Hannah used to think he could fix anything wrong in town. If only it were true.

"This kid almost did, but he was too late," said Nick. A shadow passed over his eyes, then he laughed a little. "Boy, he was mad. He turned so red I thought his head would explode."

"He'd been out running, Nick," Hannah said. "He was just hot." Martin hadn't been nice to her, but she couldn't help defending him. He wasn't there to defend himself.

"So, you know him?" A.J. asked. "He go nuts like that all the time?"

"I never heard him say a word before. Not even in class."

"Guess he finally had something to say," Hannah's mother said. "When someone who doesn't usually talk says something, you'd better listen."

"Wait a minute," said A.J. "He's a little crazy-haired kid, maybe Puerto Rican, runs a lot, new in town? He's got to be related to Michelle Medina over in Brynwood Estates. She has some orphan living with her now."

"I don't think he's an orphan," said Hannah.

"Whatever. I heard her chewing him out about something or other when we were over there doing her yard the other day. Poor kid. It's bad enough dealing with that woman and her precious lawn once a week, much less living with her."

After dinner Hannah escaped to her attic bedroom. She shivered, switched on the electric radiator, and crawled beneath the worn comforter. Vincent Vaughan Gogh kneaded the blanket beneath his feet, claws digging lightly into Hannah's flesh below.

Scritch scratch.

Hannah jumped at the noise behind her head. She knew it was a just a branch from the hemlock tree scratching the roof shingles. A.J. should have trimmed it back by now—Hannah's mother had been nagging him to get out the clippers for weeks. The noise used to scare her sometimes when she was little, but it was just an overgrown tree. She flicked her eyes toward the dormer window under the eaves. Nothing visible but deepest darkness under the dense, prickly reach of the hemlock.

Just her imagination. Just a tree. Just like the Spirit Tree. There was no such thing as curses. Whatever she thought had happened earlier—it couldn't have happened.

Scritch scratch.

Just a tree. Trees don't talk. They don't glow. They don't ask for help.

She dug her mobile phone out of her bag, bracing herself as she fired up the power.

No messages. Hannah almost laughed. What had she expected? A text from the tree? No. Not only was that impossible, she was out of airtime. If a tree wanted to contact her, it would have to wait in line behind Waverly, who managed to burn up Hannah's meager allotment of minutes within the first week of each month.

Turning the tiny ruby studs in her ears, Hannah wondered what would have happened if her best friend had been with her earlier. Would she have defended Martin? Would she have stuck around long enough to witness the storm and, well, whatever had happened? She wasn't sure she would have.

Hannah tried to do her homework, but the *scritch-scratching* of the tree sounded like it was inside her skull. Like it was trying to tell her something. Maybe even like it was trying to get in the room.

She remembered how her mother had asked her if she was sure she didn't mind moving upstairs all alone. Hannah had shaken her head. She might have shrieked over sleepover-party ghost stories, but Hannah had never believed in ghosts, monsters, or things that went bump in the night. And if she had, she would have risked the wrath of a thousand ghosts for her own space away from her brothers. They tended to fill the house, even when they weren't home.

Scritch scratch CRACK!

A branch crashed against the window, splintering the pane into a starburst of shards.

Vincent Vaughan Gogh leaped from Hannah's lap and fled down the stairs. Hannah stayed frozen in place. She was alone.

Alone except for the tree outside her window.

Heart racing, she steeled herself. It was just the same tree that had been there before she was born. She tentatively approached the window, ducking her head to fit under the sloped ceiling. The broken glass, delicate as frost, stood in place in the peeling wooden frame. She peered through the starry glass web. The nearest hemlock branch hung motionless, four feet clear of the window. Not a needle trembled. If there had been any wind a moment before, it had died to an eerie calm.

Hannah tried to remember if the window had been broken before—her mom had complained that windows kept cracking whenever the house settled. She'd tell her father, and he'd tape up the glass to hold it in place and keep drafts at bay until he got a chance to replace it. Yes, she thought. The window might have been partly broken already. She hadn't noticed, but it must have been. There wasn't even any wind.

Then Hannah heard the noise again.

Scritch scratch.

Prickles rose along her hairline. If there was no wind, what was moving the branches? She nervously appraised the angled ceiling above her head—a lumpy old crack was visible through the painted-over wallpaper, but it looked strong enough to protect her from a falling hemlock tree. At least, she hoped so.

Scritch scratch. Whatever was causing the noise, it was real. That message the Spirit Tree sent in the forest had been real. Was this a message, too?

Hannah had always trusted her senses—observe, analyze, move, no hesitation. When someone needed help, she gave it, whether that someone was a person, an animal, or even a tree. It didn't matter if she was scared. She wouldn't let anything frighten her from doing what was right—especially not a pile of sticks. And if that meant she had to lift a curse, she would. She gulped in air, the first deep breath she'd taken all afternoon.

She would listen to Martin. They would both listen to the Spirit Tree.

The scratching stopped, and the room was quiet. Hannah was ready to believe.

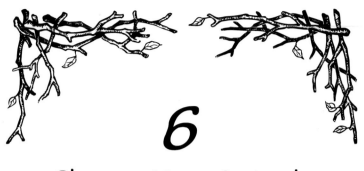

6

Change Your Attitude

Martin tried to open the heavy fiberglass door. Deadbolted. He rang the bell, and Aunt Michelle answered it, a wireless headset in her ear and a laptop balanced on her hipbone.

"I forgot you were out. Ugh, what happened to you?" she said, nose wrinkling as she took in Martin's dripping clothes and mud-caked sneakers. "Put those sneakers outside."

He tossed them and tiptoed in. She curled her lip. "Oh, now you're leaving wet footprints on the hardwood."

"Sorry. Can I use your computer?" Martin didn't have his own system. He didn't even have his own cell phone, despite the fact that Aunt Michelle was a telecommunications executive for a company that gave free mobile service to employees' immediate family. She told him that as a second cousin he didn't qualify, and she'd set a bad example for everyone at Horizon Network Communications if she stretched the rules. Aunt Michelle was a stickler for rules and technicalities.

No wonder she was so quick to tell everyone she wasn't really his aunt, but his mother's cousin. She only agreed to take Martin in because his mom was deployed overseas with the Army, and then his grandmother died. "Gone," Aunt Michelle said with a dramatic heavenward glance, but he didn't believe she really missed Abuelita like he and his mom did.

Martin's dad was gone, too, but Florida wasn't exactly heaven, though sometimes it seemed as far. Martin's dad sent his monthly checks without fail, but when Martin's mom asked if he could take their son for a few months, it turned out the house in Orlando was too small because of his new half-brother. That was fine with Martin, because as a seventh-grader, the last thing he wanted was a grubby little kid touching his stuff.

He hadn't figured Aunt Michelle would feel the same way about him.

Her temple twitched as she looked him up and down, and he felt even sweatier and muddier than before. "Get showered, then you have five minutes," she said. "I've got a ton of work."

A few minutes later, his hair in damp locks but his body clean and dry, Martin sat in the glow of the computer screen. His two index fingers hovered above the keyboard. How could he even begin to describe his day?

His mother's IM account was inactive. Martin frowned. It would have been nice knowing that his mom was on the other end of the computer, even around the world, but email would have to do. She'd read it later.

HI MOM, he typed. I MADE A COUPLE NEW FRIENDS TODAY. She didn't need to know that one was a girl who detested him and the other was a tree that might be trying to kill him. Not to mention the bad one the tree had warned about, which could be the tree itself, as far as he knew. WE'RE WORKING ON A NATURE PROJECT TOGETHER. I RAN SIX MILES BUT I GOT INTERRUPTED BY A RAINSTORM SO I DON'T KNOW MY TIME. I MISS YOU. I LOVE YOU. *Come home safe*, he thought, but didn't type.

Send. He waited a moment to see if a message pinged back, but nothing did.

Then a chat window popped open. For a split second he thought it was his mom, but the screen name was blank. Who was it? He waited for a moment, but no words appeared.

"Are you done yet?" his aunt called. "I have to finish my spreadsheets."

"I'm finished." Martin closed the window, a little sadder. Just a bug in the chat software. "What's for dinner?"

"Help yourself to what's in the freezer."

Martin heard the sprinklers pop up outside, despite the earlier rainstorm. In September other Lower Brynwood lawns were scorched dry, but Martin's aunt had the greenest lawn in the development, so bright and manicured that it looked fake. Every day at six o'clock, the sprinklers sprayed a rainbow of chlorinated town water onto the velvety grass and any kid unlucky enough to be riding his bike past.

Aunt Michelle peered out the window at the lawn, looking satisfied for a moment. Then, as if struck by a sudden rage, she shouted, "That grass is four feet if it's an inch! I don't care if it *is* some rare native species. It's an eyesore!"

Martin craned his neck to peer out the window at the perfect, green carpet of lawn. "I think the landscapers are coming tomorrow."

Aunt Michelle looked at him as if she had forgotten he was there. "Not my grass, Martin. The weed patch around that hideous shack. You have to know what I'm talking about." She pointed a manicured finger.

Through the window Martin could just make out a weathervane on the highest gable of a stone cottage—the same one with the tangled laundry and overgrown roses.

"Um, aren't you in charge of Brynwood Estates? Can't you make her mow?"

Aunt Michelle scowled at him, her temple pulsing like a drum beat. Martin recognized that temper—his mom had it, and so did he. He ought to know better than to push her, but sometimes he couldn't help himself. "I *am* the president of the Brynwood Estates Community Association, thank you very much," Aunt Michelle said. "But the cottage isn't part of it. It was the old gatehouse for the original estate, and now it's Jenna Blitzer's. She *says* it's a wildlife garden, but I know that's just another way to say 'I don't respect my neighbors.'" She flipped the blinds closed. "But she will. I have the power in my hands."

She flounced into her office, clicking the door shut behind her.

Martin nuked a diet frozen dinner and ate it standing up at the counter while a second entrée rotated on the microwave carousel. The pasta, way too hot and tasting like melted plastic, burned the roof of his mouth, but he didn't slow down. He remembered when his mom bought him *Dragon Era* right before she deployed. She'd played it with him a few times. He had totally dominated the game at Gord's house, but his mom outmaneuvered him every time, goading his ranger into false steps. She said you can't let your emotions rule you when the stakes are high. When you get angry, you make mistakes.

Out in the woods today, he'd let his anger get away from him, and that made him madder. He was neck-deep in a curse, when the last thing he had planned was to get involved. He was a short-termer in the miserable town. No use making friends.

The microwave dinged, and he sighed. He already knew another itty-bitty meal wouldn't fill the empty hole in his gut. Probably nothing would tonight.

When Martin woke in the morning, he felt as if he were being watched.

Aunt Michelle never put blinds on *his* window—just a flowery chintz swag at the top that did nothing for privacy and less for looks, in Martin's opinion. But his opinion didn't matter, since he slept on a narrow brass daybed surrounded by plastic bins of out-of-season women's shoes and clothes. The spare room was no longer spare, but did double duty as his bedroom. Aunt Michelle still needed one of the other bedrooms for her elliptical trainer and weight-training equipment, and she kept the fourth bedroom lavishly decorated for real guests.

Martin covered his head with the thin coverlet. He knew there was nothing outside the window but a bare-limbed cherry tree. He had never thought a tree could watch him, but now he wasn't sure. Dryads, serewoods, wild sylvans— they were supposed to be mythological creatures, but now he wasn't ruling any of them out.

He knew what had happened the day before wasn't a dream. Nobody really dreamed about talking trees. They dreamed about exams they hadn't studied for, forgetting to wear pants to class, losing their baseball glove before a big game, or maybe—on a good day—opening the door and seeing their mom, smiling with bags full of presents.

The blender was whirring when Martin went down to the kitchen—Aunt Michelle's breakfast smoothie. He grabbed a box of Bran Buds from the cabinet and poured them in a bowl. It looked like something a squirrel would eat, but he already knew this was the best option. He poured the milk, sighed at its thin blue tinge, and shook a yellow packet of artificial sugar granules on top. He chewed glumly, trying to finish as quickly as possible.

"Martin, you're never going to have a good day if you go around with a face like that."

"It's the face I was born with—what else can I do?"

"You know what I mean," Aunt Michelle snapped. Then she brightened, like she was pouring artificial sugar right into her voice. "If you put energy out into the world and expect it to come back to you, it will. How do you think I became vice-president of Horizon Network Communications, president of the Brynwood Estates Community Association, chairwoman of the Junior Executives of Tomorrow, and now head of the Brynwood Garden Club, too? It's about your attitude, mister. Change your attitude, change your life."

He smiled, his mouth still full of milk.

"That's better. You don't have to mean it at first. Change the way you look, and you'll change your outlook." Martin's eyes bulged a bit as he tried hard not to roll them. Aunt Michelle couldn't open her mouth without some corny saying spilling out. He swallowed the last mouthful and stood to put the bowl in the dishwasher.

"Speaking of change," he said, "can I have money for lunch?"

"I packed your lunch. You don't want those greasy burgers they serve in the cafeteria."

Yes, I do, Martin thought. He gathered his things and headed for the door.

"Best be off," he said. "Early bird and all that."

"That's the attitude."

When he'd shut the door behind him, he peeked inside the oddly light lunch bag—some kind of stinky, brownish spread on rice cakes. Might as well eat the bag. He'd have to dip into his allowance again for lunch. He'd never be able to buy his own computer at this rate.

When he looked up, Hannah was staring him right in the face. She'd been waiting on the stoop, and all of a sudden breakfast with Aunt Michelle didn't seem so bad.

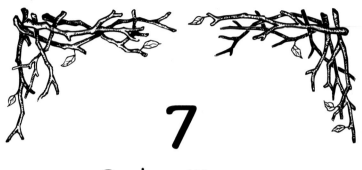

7

Bad to Worse

"I decided you need my help," Hannah said. She didn't plan to tell him about the tree branch that had cracked her window the night before. In the light of day, it would just sound silly. As if things in Lower Brynwood didn't break, crumble, and decay every day! Half the houses on her block were practically falling down already.

Martin jammed a brown bag into his backpack and zipped it up securely, as if she was likely to steal it. She had thought he'd be glad to see her, but apparently she guessed wrong.

"You skipped out," Martin answered. "I don't need you."

She winced inwardly—she took pride in making quick decisions, but she'd needed a little time for this situation. A girl didn't run into talking trees every day. But now that she was here, she wasn't going to change her mind. She was going to change *his*.

"Yeah, you do," she said. "I figured out where you lived, didn't I? I know this town, and if anybody can figure out where the curse came from, I can."

"What, you know all the dark mages in Lower Deadwood?" He started walking down the long drive, and she went with him.

"The whats?"

He snorted. "Mages. Wizards. Witches. Curseworkers. The Spirit Tree asked for our help. Whoever set this curse has got to be working some kind of dark magic."

"I don't believe in magic."

"If you don't believe, I can do this without you," Martin said, squaring his shoulders, which had been lopsided under the weight of one backpack strap. "I work best alone, anyway."

"That's not up to you. I was there, too." Hannah thought of the tree's message. *Heal me*, it had said. "The tree needs me, too." The town was counting on her. Not to mention her brother. And her own scholarship dreams, come to think of it.

"I guess I can't stop you. But you'd better get going. The bus will be here any minute." At the end of the driveway he turned toward the corner.

Hannah put her hand on his shoulder to stop him. "You don't have to ride the bus, you know. School is a five-minute walk if you know the shortcuts. None of these dumb cul-de-sacs connect, so the bus ride takes forty minutes and drags you all over town."

"I like to get an early start." He jerked his head in the direction of the house. "Aunt Michelle is doing Pilates in the living room."

Hannah couldn't imagine her own aunt exercising, but she knew she wouldn't want to watch her do it. "Okay, but skip the bus today. We need to talk, and I can't take my bike on the bus."

"Precisely."

"Fine. Waverly's dad is driving me, anyway."

"Then what's the bike for?"

"How else would I get to Waverly's house?" she said. He quirked an eyebrow at her. Riding her bike to catch a ride with Waverly's dad had always made sense to Hannah, but doubt flashed through her mind. She really went through a lot of trouble just to walk into school with Waverly, didn't she?

"You'd better get going, then," Martin said, popping in his earbuds.

Hannah raised her voice. "Meet me after school! At the Spirit Tree."

He shook his head. "I'll wait at the west exit."

"Okay. But don't be surprised if I pretend I don't know you until then."

A yellow bus rounded the corner, nearly empty at the beginning of its route. The door slid open like an accordion, and Martin climbed the steps without a word. Hannah wasn't sure if he'd heard the last part of what she said, but she was sorry she said it.

He scowled at her with one last look over his shoulder.

Yep, he heard it.

Hannah sat back on the high leather seats of the SUV, unconsciously turning the ruby studs in her ears. She had begged her mother to let her get her ears pierced when Waverly did, right before fifth grade. When Mrs. Wiggins took them to the mall together, Hannah had pretended to be as scared as Waverly acted. She had really felt nothing but excitement—it was a girl thing, and she was part of it.

The dull red and gold earrings Hannah wore now were the same ones she got that first Christmas—a reward for following instructions, turning her earrings constantly and dousing the wounds with hydrogen peroxide. Waverly's lobes had gotten infected and swollen, but that hadn't stopped her from amassing a wardrobe of earrings that filled a rack, pair by sparkling pair.

Hannah thought Waverly would be mad at her after their phone argument, but she had found a stream of apologetic voice mails on the family's machine. The first time stamp was from before she had even gotten to the Spirit Tree. Each message pitched more desperate than the last, Waverly begging for forgiveness for leaving Hannah to do something by herself. Thank goodness. Placating Waverly was one thing Hannah didn't want to worry about this morning.

"Do you believe in curses, Dr. Wiggins?" Hannah kept peeking over her shoulder, but the only thing she saw behind them was the front wheel of her bike spinning in the bike rack whenever the SUV went over a bump.

"I'm not proud of it, but words slip out now and then when somebody cuts me off in traffic," he said.

"Not that kind of curse. Bad luck and eternal misery—that sort of thing."

"Don't tell me you girls have been experimenting with that stuff," he said. His glasses glinted at her in the rearview mirror. "A lot of girls went through that witchy phase when I was young, but it's a waste of time."

"Please, Dad," Waverly interrupted. "We have better things to do."

Hannah ignored her. "How do you know witchcraft is a waste of time?"

Dr. Wiggins laughed. "Well, if anybody had been trying out love potions on me, I would have had an easier time getting a date to the senior prom."

"Come on, Dad," Waverly said. Dr. Wiggins pulled the SUV into the Lower Brynwood Middle School drop-off line. Not that this line of questioning was going anywhere. Dr. Wiggins wasn't a witch doctor—he was an optometrist. He often joked that he only believed what he could see with his own two eyes. Hannah felt the same way, but she had experienced something crazy at the Spirit Tree herself, and she barely believed it.

"You know, Hannah, I'd be happy to pick you up at your house," he said as he detached the bright pink bike from the car's rack.

"I don't want to be any trouble. Besides, I need my bike to get home after soccer practice."

"Then why don't you just ride your bike all the way to school? You were only in the car for three blocks."

Waverly shook her head. "If she did that, we wouldn't be able to walk into school together." Hannah shrugged. She had never noticed that, for an only child, Waverly sure hated to be alone.

"Silly me," said Dr. Wiggins, climbing back into the driver's seat. He knew better than to hug Waverly goodbye in front of the school. Hannah raised her hand when she caught him waving out the window, but if Waverly saw him, she didn't show any sign. Instead she just slouched by the bike rack as Hannah threaded the lock around the steel tubes.

A bus disgorged a flow of kids. Waverly didn't bother to move, but Hannah thought she spied Martin, pushed along in the human tide. She halfway lifted her hand to wave, but he was gone, if he had been there at all.

At the beginning of social studies she realized she was on the receiving end of the silent treatment, and she didn't like it. Martin was ignoring her. She'd never fully registered his presence in class before, but he sat just a few rows from her. He wouldn't look at her, just sat with his iPod on, doodling some kind of hideous tree demon in his notebook. He whipped off his earbuds before Mr. Michaelson came through the door. As usual, Martin never raised his hand during class—no wonder. They were in the middle of a unit on state and local history, and there was no way Martin could be prepared. Hannah's hand shot into the air at nearly every question, but Mr. Michaelson only called on her whenever no one else seemed to know the answer.

"Can anyone explain our town's original name?" His eyes flicked over the class, which looked half-asleep. "Hannah?"

"The town was named for the first mayor, Thomas Brynwood, who had been a garrison officer for George Washington and owned land in the area," she said.

Mr. Michaelson shook his head and looked at her over his rimless glasses. "That's true, but this area has only been called Brynwood since 1897. I was talking about the *original* name. Anyone else?"

"Millville," Martin said, as if it had just occurred to him out of the blue. "I saw it on one of those green history signs in the park. I guess it was named for a mill."

"That's right. Millville was known for production of flour in Thomas Brynwood's time, as well as gunpowder and textiles. The town was renamed in the charter-holder's honor during the one-hundredth anniversary of its incorporation after the war," said Mr. Michaelson. "Next time, raise your hand, Mr. Cruz."

Hannah turned to stare down Martin, annoyed that he'd answered the question she missed. Now he finally looked at her, sideways, with a little smile. Was he mocking her? They were supposed to be in this together. She decided to look on the bright side. At least he wasn't as clueless as she'd first thought.

The day passed way too slowly, and yet Hannah deliberately sidled through the west exit doors fifteen minutes after the final bell rang. Martin stood next to her bike, his iPod on and his hands jammed into his pockets.

"I wasn't sure you were coming," he said, his eyes narrowed in the bright September sunshine as he popped his earbuds out.

"I keep my word. It took a while to lose Waverly. Usually we hang out if I don't have soccer practice, but I'm not sure she's ready for, well, this situation."

"Like you were ready," Martin snorted.

"True. I haven't spent as much time as you pretending to be an elf and talking to trees." She glared at him, and neither of them blinked. At last Hannah sighed and said, "Ready or not, we should head back to the Spirit Tree and see what we can find out."

"Great. We can interrogate the tree," Martin said. "If the tree can send messages, maybe it can answer them, too."

Hannah gave him a dismissive look as she secured her messenger bag to the back of the bike. "You ask the questions. In the meantime, there are plenty of clues right in the carvings. We don't need any magic for that—just observation and logic."

"Yeah, I'm sure there's an instruction manual written on the bark."

Hannah concentrated on unlocking her bike to avoid another staring contest. "We've got to use whatever we've got," she said through gritted teeth. "If the tree has an operator standing by, we'll ask questions. Otherwise, we'll look at the clues carved in the bark."

"Fair enough."

Hannah heaved her bike from the rack and started to walk beside it, but Martin threw his second backpack strap over his shoulder. "You can ride," he said. "I'll run."

"It's pretty far."

"I'm pretty fast."

"Fine." Hannah swung a leg over the seat and pushed off first, but Martin accelerated more quickly and caught up. She could already hear Martin breathing next to her—

not winded, just the rhythmic exhalations of a practiced runner, his sinewy arms pumping in time. He had put his earbuds in and grasped the iPod in his left hand. A little rude, she thought, but she liked music when she ran, too. He seemed to be in his own world, staring straight ahead, but she kept stealing glances over at him, wanting to say something. After all, they were supposed to be together. At last she couldn't stand the silence.

"How much do you run, anyway?" she asked, loudly so he could hear her over whatever he was listening to.

He didn't look at her. "Forty or fifty miles a week."

Hannah whistled.

Martin grinned, the same little sudden smile he had flashed her in social studies. She couldn't help smiling back.

"I'm training," Martin huffed, "for a marathon…with my mom."

"Your mom? But I thought…"

"She's in Afghanistan. She trains on a treadmill—the roads are too dangerous there. But when she gets back, we're going to run a race together."

"Which one?" Hannah shifted gears and pedaled a little harder as they hit an incline.

Martin didn't slow down at the hill, but loud breaths punctuated his speech. "Don't know…started training for a 5k…then a 10k…then a half-marathon…didn't get to do them…but now we're ready…for the big one…whenever she comes back."

Hannah's mother was barely ready for a walk around the block these days. Sometimes she embarrassed her daughter with her ever-expanding butt, but Hannah couldn't imagine not seeing her for months—even years.

"And you don't have to shout," he said. "I can hear you just fine."

The streets of the Brynwood Estates passed underneath them, winding in circles and dead-end cul-de-sacs.

"Stop." Hannah's brakes squealed, and Martin ran into her back tire. "The witch's house." She pointed. "You're supposed to stop here and count as high as you can until you get scared. Waverly and I used to dare each other, but now I just like to look at it."

From the street, the first floor of the brownstone cottage was barely visible behind the thicket of tumbling blue and purple asters and fountains of yellow maiden grass. The grand wrought-iron gate stood open, tall enough to reach the second floor of the cottage, but a tangle of bittersweet and honeysuckle had made a trellis of the rusted swirls. The thickness of the vines proved the gates hadn't swung shut in many years. The driveway between them was cracked asphalt, lined on either side with granite blocks, continuing past the cottage and ending in a pile of rubble at the willow fence that demarcated the back garden. Once, Hannah knew, the road must have continued for nearly a half-mile to Brynwood Hall, the old mansion where Thomas Brynwood himself had lived after the Revolutionary War, when he was a rich old man and the town's founder. Now the only thing back there was the high-school athletic fields.

"That's Jenna Blitzer's place," Martin said.

"What?" Hannah slid off the seat and put her feet flat on the pavement.

"I thought you knew everything about this town."

"I do. Everybody calls this the witch's house, like Hansel and Gretel."

"I thought you didn't believe in magic." He bent over and rested his hands on his knees, still breathing heavily—proof that he was human, and not a robot after all.

"I don't!" She could feel her face getting hot and hoped she wasn't as red as Martin. "Nobody believes she's a witch—well, nobody over the age of eight."

"My Aunt Michelle would bulldoze the whole place under if she could. Jenna's exempt from the Brynwood Estates Community Association rules."

Hannah considered the house, twisting the ruby in her right ear. "It's spooky, but I always liked it."

"Me, too," said Martin, grinning. "I like anything that drives Aunt Michelle crazy."

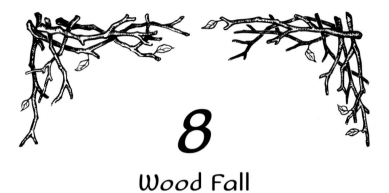

8

Wood Fall

The trail through Brynwood Park ran parallel to Mill Creek, the shallow run that had carved the valley and once powered Thomas Brynwood's mill, according to the sign at the park entrance. The running path, uneven from erosion, seemed steeper to Martin today, now that he was walking instead of running. He noticed flattened soda cans and plastic bags caught in the brush and wished he were alone instead of with a bossy girl.

"I'm going to run the rest of the way," he said, and took off. He felt like a ranger again, running through the trees, practically leaping from trunk to trunk like a squirrel. The place was magical. Dark magic, light magic—it didn't matter.

The water gurgled musically over the flat rocks, and as Martin climbed he imagined himself flowing up as the water flowed down. The saplings growing on either side of the creek stretched upward, nearly meeting at the center as they reached for the sun, away from the dappled shadow of the canopy sixty feet above them. And there was the Spirit Tree before him, its branches spread open like the fingers of a skeletal hand grasping at the sky.

The woods seemed less ominous under blue skies, but Martin still worried about what he'd find—more glowing messages, maybe. But he didn't expect the scene before him. The ground around the Spirit Tree was littered with broken branches, from twigs to heavy limbs. The tree had nearly shattered since they had been there.

He tore through the debris, tripping through the tangle of brush to get to the beech. He had barely touched the trunk when he heard Hannah behind him. She moved faster than he thought she would; he had forgotten she was a soccer player.

"I guess the lightning did more damage than we thought," Hannah said. She picked up a fallen branch, gently stroking the yellowing leaves as if they were cat's ears. She looked up, and Martin followed her gaze. Most of the leaves overhead were still green, but straw-colored leaves flagged some of the branches.

An ear-splitting noise tore through the silence. Part of the canopy crashed toward them with startling speed. Hannah and Martin dove out of the way of a thick branch.

"Holy crap," Martin said, splayed out on the ground. This was the second time the tree had knocked him down in as many days. That tree was cursed, all right.

He straightened himself up and reached out a hand to Hannah. She seemed dazed and oblivious to the mud soaking into the back of her jeans. The branch had driven itself into the wet ground right where they had been standing. It could have killed them. Martin looked up—was it an accident? A message? Was the bad one playing games with them?

"That branch could have taken our heads off," said Hannah. She stood and brushed off her muddy butt with one hand, still gently holding the green twig with the other. "You don't think the Spirit Tree meant to hurt us, do you?"

"I don't think so. It's the tree that's hurt," Martin said. Had the tree felt pain when the limb tore off? He hoped not.

"It looks pretty bad today—like it's dying," Hannah said. She tucked the twig into her bag.

"The curse is getting worse. Once the tree's dead, it's dead," Martin said, a familiar disquiet creeping through his body. There was no trace of light in the tree. He thought of his grandmother's body, waxy in its coffin, cold to his last kiss. His mom had held him by the shoulders while he cried—back home on a bereavement leave that was way too short. His grandmother was gone. His mother was gone again, and he was stuck here with Aunt Michelle. Dead was dead.

"It's not dead yet," Hannah said, jolting him out of his thoughts. "Maybe we can heal it before it's too late. That's why we're here."

Martin eyed the tree up and down, from its gnarled roots to the yellowing leaves. It didn't look good, but it was the same tree he had tried to save yesterday. Maybe the Spirit Tree wasn't quite a friend, but it was his ally. His wild sylvan, even if it had almost dropped a branch on his head. Accidents happened.

"Right. So, let's get started," he said at last.

"Okay," Hannah said. "I'll take notes. You can go ahead any time."

Martin looked at her, not sure what she was expecting him to do.

"Aren't you going to interrogate it?" she said, raising her eyebrows like a challenge.

Martin didn't know how to begin. *O mighty tree, tell us your secrets.* He'd sound like a lunatic. Or at least like some kind of live-action, role-playing loser. Which he was sometimes, but Hannah didn't have to know it. Instead he said, "Um, Hannah, let's try this your way. Notes first."

"Okay. We have a trunkload of leads right there in the carvings, if we can figure them out." She looked warily up to where the tree met the sky, maybe checking for more falling branches, then took a notebook and pen out of her messenger bag. "When my parents were growing up, Lower Brynwood was a good place to live. Better than Upper Brynwood, maybe. More fun. But something changed. Everyone thought the factories closing started all our bad luck, but what if the curse really started the troubles? What if *it* caused everything to collapse here?"

Martin shivered. He told himself that it was just evaporating sweat, not fear. "Maybe. But why? And how?"

"Let's think." Hannah chewed one side of her mouth. "So, why would someone curse something—a person, a tree, whatever?"

"Usually revenge," said Martin. Then he thought of the sorcerer clans in *Dragon Era*, and remembered how the Worlinzer sorceresses laid brutal curses that could drain a ranger's skill points, then turn around and use his talents against him. There was nothing worse than facing an enemy armed with powers they'd just stolen. "Or maybe to get something for themselves."

"Okay," said Hannah. "So, we're looking for someone with a grudge against Lower Brynwood, or a person with something to gain if the town went down the tubes."

"If we figure out when the curse started, then we can find out what happened around the same time—who stole whose husband, who hit the bingo jackpot at St. Barnabas. Who lost and who won," said Martin.

"Right!" Hannah's ponytail whipped back and forth as she got excited. "And that's how we'll find the guilty party."

The bad one, Martin thought. Did he really want to find somebody who was capable of slinging curses in real life? He swallowed. "So, when did the Spirit Tree tradition start? That's probably our best bet."

"I don't know, exactly," Hannah said, flipping to a blank page. "My mom said they didn't do it when she was young. So if we find the oldest carving, we'll find out when the curse started."

"Yeah!" Martin said. "Maybe even something that tells us who set it—a witch's mark or something. A signature. A rune. Look, I didn't tell you before, but after you left, the tree called someone *the bad one*. If we find the bad one, we can figure out how to stop them."

Hannah cocked her head. "Is there anything else you didn't tell me?"

"I wasn't holding out on you—you left me here, remember?" Martin felt himself getting hot again, despite his damp T-shirt.

"I won't do it again—we're a team now," she said, as if a team were the most sacred thing in the world. She hesitated, and he waited for her to say something. She shook her head, as if shaking a thought away. She pointed to Martin's earbuds, still on either side of his head. "Do you have a camera on that thingie?"

"What?" Martin whipped off the iPod, reaching behind him as if he were double-jointed to shove it into his backpack before she could grab it. "No. It's really old."

"I have my mom's camera. I'll take pictures, you take notes—write down everything you see, like a scientific field journal. Right now we won't know what's important and what's not."

Martin jumped the first time the flash went off, thinking the lightning had returned, but they soon settled into a rhythm punctuated by the strobe of the camera. He sketched a diagram and tried to replicate the marks he saw, position and all.

"I can't read half these carvings," he said. As the tree had grown, natural cracks and texture in the bark had obliterated some letters. There was some bad handiwork, too. Clearly those kids had never been Boy Scouts—or scholars, either.

"Then just draw what you see. Maybe it will make sense later," Hannah said.

Rock on, class of 2004. Party like it's 1999. In between the class sayings were random graffiti—names and bands and professions of love with creative spelling. *Van Halen. MJ + JB. I luv Jake. U2 4ever. To Brynwood 1997.*

Martin felt more and more disgusted. Who really wanted to immortalize such ridiculous sayings?

Hannah cringed.

"What? What did you see?" Martin asked. She pointed to the fresh words overlapping two of the oldest carvings— *Lo-B Rulz.*

"I can't believe I came here to be part of the ceremony yesterday," she said. "Now it just seems stupid." Her shoulders sagged. Then she said, "How about you? Find anything like a curse?"

"A few four-letter words, but nothing I don't see in the boys' bathroom every day," he said, hoping she'd know he was joking.

She laughed, and he smiled. "You should see the girls' room," she said. "Maybe you'd better not. So, what's the oldest carving you found?"

He scanned his list. "Looks like 1990."

"Ha!" She held up her notebook like she just won at bingo. "I've got 1989—*Forever young, 9/15/89.*"

The sun went behind a cloud and Martin shivered. "Sounds like something written on a gravestone."

"Hey, take a look at this!" Hannah called out. Martin bent toward the carving beneath her finger. The bark had healed over, almost obscuring the figures, but the repeated symbol was still visible. "Could this be a code? Like the sign of the devil?"

"The sign of the devil is three sixes. This is six threes," Martin said.

"I said a code. Or maybe the person who made it is dyslexic. These threes are backwards," said Hannah.

"That's because they're not threes. They're Es," he said, tracing the crude letters.

"Like an eye chart?" Hannah said. "See, there's a big one on top, then smaller ones in rows underneath."

"Maybe," Martin said. "But why would a witch put an eye chart on a tree?"

Hannah shrugged. "Waverly's dad is an optometrist. I'll ask him about it tomorrow."

Martin was about to argue when he heard something large crashing through the brush—the sound was definitely too big to be a squirrel. He braced for another invader.

Hannah didn't look surprised when a tall blond guy appeared. Hannah's brother. Crap. Martin had hoped never to see him again. At least his thug teammates weren't with him.

"You came!" Hannah said, running up as if to hug him. The blond guy grinned, tossing his leather bag down to slip her into a headlock and ruffle her hair like a puppy's fur. He nodded at Martin, who didn't make eye contact, assessing the dangerous-looking implements that had fallen from the bag. What were those—loppers? A hand saw? Was he planning to take the whole tree down today?

"What's *he* doing here?" Martin said, trying to talk tough and ranger-like but sounding whiny even to his own ears.

"I asked him to stop by. He can help us heal the tree," Hannah said.

"He's done enough already." Martin clenched his fists. What could this dumb football player do other than mess things up even worse?

Hannah's brother shook his shaggy, streaky head. "Nick wasn't kidding about this kid," he said to Hannah, as if Martin couldn't hear. "He's like a little Tasmanian Devil."

Hannah threw her hands up, as if to signal that she thought Martin was crazy, too. Of course she'd be on her brother's side. Martin glared at them both, and then Hannah laughed.

"It's okay, Martin. This isn't Nick. This is our older brother, A.J. He graduated two years ago. He's a landscaper."

"I'm your aunt's landscaper," A.J. said, pointing to the logo on his forest-green T-shirt. "I work for Laughlin Landscaping and Tree Care."

Martin's eyes widened in recognition, then embarrassment. "Oh. Sorry, man." The brothers could've been twins.

"You should be sorry," Hannah said. "He's going to help us figure out what's wrong with the tree. We don't know anything about plants, and he does. And the tree is in worse shape than we thought."

"No kidding. What happened in the last two years?" A.J. asked, sizing the tree up. "That thing looks like kindling."

"That's why I asked you to come. We need to act now to save it. It's part of our town's history." She turned her wide eyes on Martin and said proudly, "A.J. studied horticulture in college."

A.J. snorted. "For a semester at the community college. Still, that makes me more qualified than my boss." He circled the tree as if he was looking for something, then stopped. He touched the letters on one inscription and read out loud, "*Victory will be ours.* I carved that. Didn't come true." He paused, then looked up. "Huh. Well, this is an American beech tree. The bark is beginning to crack and blister, not just around the carvings, but all up and down the trunk."

"I don't remember seeing that yesterday," said Hannah, squinting.

"Huh." He pushed back his floppy hair and scratched his head. "Looks like some kind of fungus or viral blight made its way into the wounds left by the carvings. I'll take some material samples and try to find out more. You got a camera?"

"Yeah," Hannah said. "Mom's."

"I hope you asked to borrow that. Anyway, get some close-ups."

Martin gritted his teeth when A.J. pulled out a pocketknife. Not again. But A.J. scraped off some of the bark thoughtfully—surgically, even. He gathered some fallen wood too, picking up a few branches and examining them closely. Hannah snapped a few more shots, then patted the bark and stepped back next to Martin.

"How about we call it a day? I think I've photographed every square inch of this trunk already." She leaned in closer to Martin and spoke softly. "Those six Es are the most interesting thing we've found so far. We might as well try to figure out what they mean before we go any further."

"I'll give you guys a ride home," A.J. said. Martin wanted to refuse, but he felt suddenly tired. A ride would be nice.

As they headed off, Martin took a last look behind him. Orange sunlight streaked through the branches. It almost looked as if the tree was lighting up again. Martin thought as loudly as he could, *O mighty tree, tell us your secrets.*

A light blazed up on the trunk for an instant, right where the cryptic carving had been. He waved goodbye, just in case the tree could see him.

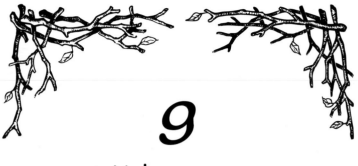

9

Volunteers

Waverly always sat next to Hannah in social studies. Usually, she didn't stop talking until Mr. Michaelson told her to, but today she seemed too fascinated by her manicure to glance at Hannah.

The night before, Hannah had called her five times, but Waverly didn't answer, which was weird. She normally got out of the shower to answer the phone—she just couldn't resist. And that morning Dr. Wiggins was the only person who spoke during the ride to school.

"I'm sorry, Wave." Hannah didn't know what she was apologizing for, but pretending to be sorry seemed like a good start.

Waverly spoke through her teeth, not looking up. "I know you didn't go to soccer after school yesterday. If you didn't want to hang out, you should've told me. You're supposed to tell me everything."

Hannah wanted to tell Waverly about the tree, but Waverly would never believe it. She wouldn't have teamed up with Martin if the whole world was at stake, much less a tree. He just wasn't her type of person.

Not for the first time, Hannah wondered if she was, either. When she was little, her mom had tried to dress her in pink dresses and bows, but as soon as she could refuse, she chose hand-me-downs from her brothers—jeans and discarded Thomas the Tank Engine knock-offs. Her mom offered her ballet lessons at the Lo-B rec center, but she chose soccer and tee-ball, just like her brothers did. And she was good. With two brothers to coach her, she never threw "like a girl." She never even understood what that expression was supposed to mean.

But when she became friends with Waverly in second grade, Hannah realized she had a lot to learn about being a girl. It seemed like Waverly had been born knowing how to layer T-shirts, pair shoes with jeans, apply lip gloss, and toss her head so that her hair caught the light.

"If you're going to play soccer with the cutest boys in school," she always said, "try to look good while you do it." Hannah suspected Waverly was a little jealous, but she didn't need to be. The last thing Hannah wanted was a boyfriend.

Mr. Michaelson walked into class, looking young and watery-eyed as he cleaned his glasses with the tail of his tie. He replaced his eyeglasses on his high-bridged nose, regaining his authoritative look as he signaled the class to quiet down. "It's time for us to begin planning our required community service projects. I'm asking you to pair up, draft proposals next Friday, then present the final project to the class in four weeks."

Martin's hand shot up.

"Do you have a question, Martin?"

"No, Mr. Michaelson. I just wanted to say that Hannah Vaughan and I will work together."

Hannah's jaw dropped. How dare he speak for her? She always worked with Waverly. Waverly finally looked at Hannah, narrowing her eyes as if she wanted to shoot laser beams out of them. Her best friend thought Hannah had planned this—that she deliberately paired with someone else! She tried to signal to Martin, but he waved her off, apparently under the impression that she was thanking him for his brilliant move. He didn't even know the trouble he'd caused.

"Very good," Mr. Michaelson said. "I take it you have a project in mind, and I can't wait to hear what you have planned."

Martin smiled. Hannah and Waverly did not.

They still weren't smiling as they pushed their way through the throng toward the cafeteria. At least, Waverly didn't smile at *Hannah*—she passed out generous, beauty-queen waves and greetings to a group of girls they passed, then dropped back into stony silence with Hannah.

Finally, Waverly said, "It's cool if you want to work with that weirdo, Hannah. You always did like pathetic little strays, like that sad cat of yours."

"Martin's not a stray. He's just new. And my cat isn't sad or pathetic."

"Okay, I take it back," she said. "I mean, the part about your cat." Waverly held her giant handbag in front of her like an expensive leather battering ram and beat a path through the hall for them both. "I'm working with Libby Cho-Johnson now, and her parents are both lawyers. They'll help us on the project. We're going to work on it at lunch. Hey, there's your new partner. Maybe you and Marvin should sit together."

"It's Martin, with a T. And yeah, I kind of do have to talk to him."

Waverly's stony demeanor crumpled. Hannah could see that she was hurt at being left out, not just mad.

"I'll tell you about it later, Wave. We're going to the game, right?"

Waverly puffed her glossy lips into a pout. She didn't nod, but she didn't say no, either. Hannah figured that was as good an answer as she was going to get.

Martin huddled at a long lunch table, crowded except for the empty seats on either side of him. Hannah sat down, but he seemed absorbed in his iPod and the huge amount of food on his tray. It looked gross to her, but he shoveled it down with obvious relish.

She tapped him on the shoulder. "Haven't eaten in a while, huh?"

"What?" He dislodged the white buds from his ears.

"You seem to be enjoying your lunch."

"Yeah, the food here is great, isn't it?" he said with his mouth full. He eyed the brown bag clutched in her hand and hunched protectively over his tray. "If you want to try something, okay, but I don't have enough to share."

"I'm not going to steal your lunch! I just want to know what you were trying to pull in social studies."

"Oh, that," he said, swallowing. "That was lucky, wasn't it? Now we have a perfect excuse."

"For what?"

"For being together."

"Nobody's going to think you're my boyfriend, if that's what you're worried about. If you think people will think we're together, you don't know how Lower Brynwood Middle works."

He reddened for a moment, then recovered, raising his voice after every few words as if talking to a very small and stupid child. "The Spirit Tree? Our community history project? We can find out about the carvings? Try to figure out how to heal it? Ask as many questions as we want? Nobody will think anything of it?"

"Oh." Hannah sighed. It did fit. Maybe she *was* a stupid child. And Martin was pretty smart, after all. "Good thinking. But Waverly's mad at me. We're always partners."

"Who's Waverly?"

"Only my best friend." At least she *was*, Hannah thought. "And the seventh-grade class president at Lower Brynwood Middle."

"What an oxymoron."

"What did you call her?" Hannah said, bristling. She had just spoken up for Martin—now she had to defend Waverly, too.

"Not moron. The school name is an oxymoron—Lower Brynwood Middle. *Lower Middle*. Like jumbo shrimp. Didn't you ever notice?"

Hannah felt even dumber, and she didn't like it one bit. Despite her lifetime of study, she was beginning to realize there was a lot about Lower Brynwood she'd never noticed. Instead she said, "I can't work on the tree project after school today. I have soccer practice, then the game."

"What game?"

Hannah looked at him as if he were insane. "The opener for the football season. Lower Brynwood against Methacton. My brother Nick is team captain. Maybe you remember that ceremony the other day?"

"I don't like high-school sports, and I'm not going to cheer on the bullies who cut the tree."

"Actually, that's why you *should* care. If the ceremony started the curse, then the game matters. Maybe the curseworker will be there."

"So *you* go," he said. He used a French fry to mop up the ketchup on his plate and popped it into his mouth.

"Wouldn't miss it. I'm supposed to be going with Waverly, if she's talking to me by then."

She almost stood to return to her usual spot next to Waverly, until she glanced over to see her best friend deep in conversation with Libby. Libby caught Hannah's eye, then looked away as if she hadn't.

Hannah sighed. She might as well sit with Martin. She took a soggy fry off his tray and ate it without asking, just to tease him.

He didn't seem mad—just pushed the dish closer so she could reach it. "Good, huh?"

And actually, it was.

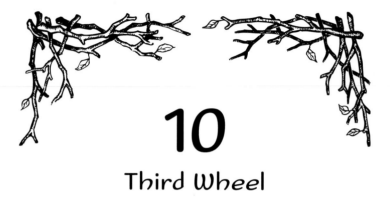

10

Third Wheel

"Oh, it's just you. Come in." Waverly left the door open and turned away. Hannah felt anything but welcome, but she stepped into the foyer before her friend changed her mind and slammed the door in her face.

"I would have called to make sure we were still on, but well, you know," Hannah said.

"No phone time. A convenient excuse, as always. So, you were off serving the community with your special friend?" Waverly kept walking, and Hannah trailed her into the sunken family room. She had looked forward to this game for weeks, and this wasn't the way she had pictured it.

"No, I had soccer," she said, pretending everything was normal between them. Hannah knew that, if she defended herself, the argument would escalate. Once, Waverly had refused to speak to Hannah for a week after Hannah had protested a rule change in the middle of the Game of Life. "But we got a lot done yesterday. A.J. came, too. He's helping us. See, we're trying to document the history of the Spirit Tree. It doesn't look so good, and A.J. knows a lot about trees."

"A.J. is helping?" Waverly's pout deflated. "You should have told me. Is he going to the game, too?"

Hannah nodded, then jumped to clarify. "He's going with his friends. We might not even see them. His girlfriend will probably be there, too." Waverly could be positively embarrassing the way she fawned over A.J., and Hannah found it best to keep them apart.

Waverly's expression turned sour again. "Well, I sure hope your buddy isn't coming to the football game with us."

"No. He doesn't like watching sports."

"I guess he'd rather dress up like a dwarf and play video games or something cool like that."

Hannah decided not to mention Waverly's addiction to the video game *Project Catwalk 4,* or the fact that she and Hannah had dressed up to match the fashions they designed more than a few times.

Waverly scowled, and Hannah wondered if she was remembering the same thing. Then Waverly said, "Well, I invited Libby. I wasn't sure you were coming. So if we talk about our project, I hope you don't feel left out."

Dr. Wiggins peered around a doorway. "I thought I heard your voice, Hannah. How's soccer going?"

She shrugged.

"Do you have any ideas for the science fair yet? I think you'd be really good at it."

"Not exactly," Hannah said. "But I do have a town history project I'm working on. Have you ever heard of the Spirit Tree?"

"Spirits in trees? Or ghost trees?"

"No, a real tree. The one in the park the high-school seniors carve mottos into."

Waverly lifted her perfectly arched eyebrows. "You two talk about trees. I'm going to let Libby know when we're picking her up." She texted furiously, thumbs flying. Hannah was sure she was writing something more than just the pickup time. Probably something not so nice about Hannah or Martin. Hannah turned her back on Waverly.

"Dr. Wiggins, would you look at something that was written on the tree?" Hannah pulled the project notebook out of her bag and flipped to the page with the strange symbols. "Is this an eye chart?"

He studied it. "Are you sure you copied this exactly?"

She nodded.

"Then it couldn't be an eye chart." He pointed at the rows of letters. "See, all the Es are facing the same way, not in different directions."

"Oh." Hannah frowned and reached for the book, but Dr. Wiggins didn't give it back. Waverly was still jabbing at her phone with her thumbs.

"Where did you say this was written?" he asked.

"The Spirit Tree."

"Doesn't ring a bell." Then he squinted and ticked off the letters, counting under his breath. A light came into his eyes. "Six Es! I remember something." He walked over to the built-in bookcases and pulled out a black leatherette book stamped in silver. "My old high-school yearbook." He flipped to the index, and then opened to a grainy black and white picture. "Here it is. Six Es: Environment, Ecology, and Energy Efficiency for an Enlightened Earth. It was a club."

He pointed at a short kid in the front with glasses so big they must have needed windshield wipers. "That's me," he said. The younger Dr. Wiggins stood next to a curly-haired girl with long earrings like chandeliers. The image was blurry, but something about her face seemed familiar.

"Who's that next to you?" Hannah asked.

"An old friend. Jenna."

Hannah looked up in surprise, then back at the girl in the photo. She was the only kid in the group not smiling.

"Jenna Blitzer? The same Jenna Blitzer who lives in that old cottage?"

"Sure is. She founded the Six Es. The only reason I joined was to be close to her, but she was serious about ecology. Everyone else thought it was just hippie talk, but Jenna was all about the science behind the environment."

"Do you think she took part in the Spirit Tree ceremony?"

"I don't remember any of that—sounds like something the Spirit Club would have cooked up. Rah-rah stuff wasn't my thing. Wasn't Jenna's, either. The only way she'd get involved would be to stop it. Save the trees, save the whales."

Hannah checked the date stamped in silver on the cover—1989. She felt electricity run through her body, like when the lightning struck the tree. That was the year of the oldest carving they had found. *Forever young, 9/15/89.* She flipped back to Jenna's stern face. She looked like a girl with a mission—but what kind of mission?

"Can I borrow this book, Dr. Wiggins? I might need it for my social studies project." She hugged the book to her body.

"I don't know how it would help, but sure. I haven't looked at it in years, anyway," he said, looking wistful. "Haven't thought much about high school, either. You and Waverly have a lot to look forward to."

Hannah gasped. "The game! We're going to miss Nick being announced."

"Let's get going, then."

In the Vaughan family, everything stopped for football.

Hannah packed the notebook and yearbook away, thinking of the Spirit Tree, ancient but dying, the record of the town's triumphs and failures, and she knew that the game wouldn't be the most important thing that had happened that week. But she still wanted to see it.

"Wait a minute," said Waverly, just as Hannah and Dr. Wiggins headed to the attached garage. She ran back upstairs and came out with a crinkled black scarf shot with silver threads.

"There," she said, stretching from the back seat into the front to drape it around Hannah's neck. "You look so cute."

"It's not cold," said Hannah, plucking at the fabric self-consciously but smiling back at her. Waverly gave no higher compliment.

"It's not supposed to keep you warm. It just ties everything together."

Hannah bit her lip. If only the mystery of the Spirit Tree were so easy.

11

Friday Night Rice

Martin left his running shoes and socks by the door. He had stepped into a huge pile of extremely pungent animal crap, and he wasn't sure he'd get the smell out. His brand-new Nikes might be passable for a weekend run, but no way would he go to school smelling like a zoo sewer. He'd be stuck wearing his old ones, which had soles that flapped at the toe. He pictured himself tripping in the cafeteria, and wondered if it was worse to look stupid or smell horrible. Life was full of difficult choices.

He noticed a striped canvas bag full of pink-handled gardening tools peeking out of the hall closet, and wondered if it held a trowel or brush to clean his running shoes. Martin slid over to take a closer look at the engraved brass tag on the tote—*Michelle Medina, President, Brynwood Garden Club.* It figured—those tools must have been purely ceremonial, like the presidency itself. Aunt Michelle would do anything for another title beside her name, and those fancy implements looked more ornamental than anything growing in her artificially green yard.

Still, she had some heavy-duty hardware in there, even if it *was* pink. Martin tested the edge of the shears and clawed at the air with the curved tines of a cultivator. If an Arlithean raider ever showed up in Brynwood Estates, Martin knew where to arm the defense.

Aunt Michelle called from the other room, "Is that you, Martin?"

He let the tools drop with a clatter. Crap, she must have heard that.

"Stop that racket and come in here for dinner," she said.

Martin could hardly believe his luck. In the kitchen, Aunt Michelle had dished Chinese takeout onto a porcelain plate and ate with chopsticks at the kitchen table. Martin's stomach growled. He would love some spicy orange-flavored beef like the kind he and Mom always bought by the quart, but any old pork fried rice or chicken lo mein would be okay. He unfolded the half-empty cartons on the counter—just white rice and overcooked steamed vegetables that shriveled as the vapor left the carton.

"Is there any soy sauce?" he asked when he sat next to Aunt Michelle, his plate brimming with dry food. What it lacked in flavor he would make up in quantity. She tossed him a single packet and went back to eating rice one grain at a time. The scented lemon-spice candle burning between them smelled more delicious than the food. Martin tore open the packet and drained every drop of brown liquid over his plate. He ignored the chopsticks and shoveled the food into his mouth with the serving spoon Aunt Michelle had left on the counter.

"Slow down, Martin," she growled, then returned to her usual fluting tones. "Eating is about satisfying appetites, but dining is a ritual. Consumption should always be a conscious activity."

"I'm really hungry," he said with his mouth full. His stomach grumbled as he tried to fill it.

She put down her chopsticks and sighed. "You'll never get anywhere in life with manners like that. Maybe that was fine at your mother's house, but here in Brynwood Estates, I expect a higher standard of behavior. And I'm going to help you achieve it."

He braced himself for what was next. Anything Aunt Michelle planned for him had to be close to torture.

"I've signed you up for an after-school activity. You'll love it—Junior Junior Executives of Tomorrow. Junior JET for short. When I was young we only had JET in high school, but that club was the first step that turned me into the successful executive I am today. It will teach you to focus on what you want, and attract people, things, and responses toward you. If you can see the power in your mind, you possess the power."

Martin scraped his plate with the giant spoon. "I can't do it. I'm working on a community history project after school."

"If you *say* you can't, then you can't." Aunt Michelle popped a single grain of rice into her mouth.

He felt a glimmer of hope. "Does that mean I don't have to do it?"

"No, that's an expression. What I meant is that you can do *both* if you really want to and set your mind to it."

Martin opened his mouth to protest that he had no intention of doing both, but Aunt Michelle shushed him.

"It's only one Thursday a week, sweetie," she said, sounding anything but sweet. "Plus Sunday nights, of course. If I had had Junior JET when I was your age, who knows how much farther I would have gone!"

Martin wished she had gone anywhere but Lower Brynwood. Just as he thought things were getting interesting, they got worse. He wanted to be out tracking the source of magic—real, live magic—but instead he was condemned to sit around with wannabe CEOs jabbering about stock prices and golf scores, or whatever that kind of kid talked about. It was his worst social nightmare—*like a curse*, he thought grimly.

He heard a rumble in the distance. At first he thought it was thunder, then realized it was the bass of a marching band. The football game would start soon. If he had any money, he'd put it on the visiting team.

12

Season Opener

Hannah sat next to Dr. Wiggins during the car ride, but that wasn't the only reason she felt like one of the adults in the car. After dressing her up, Waverly had ignored her as soon as Libby opened the car door. They jabbered together about their project, which was supposed to be a history of the Brynwood Park Mall. Every now and then they fell silent, and Hannah could hear the click of thumbs on cell-phone buttons, punctuated by giggles.

Hannah felt her face get hot. She unwrapped the scarf and crossed her arms. The Brynwood Park Mall wasn't even a real mall. It was just a shopping strip next to the closed-down Walmart and Happy Elf Bakery. If that's what passed for a historic landmark in Lower Brynwood, she didn't know if the place was worth saving. She and Martin would be better off rescuing some more worthy town.

Now Hannah was cold in the blast of the A/C. She twined the scarf around her neck, trying to imitate the way Waverly had tied it, but she got it all wrong. The stadium lights glowed in the orange and purple twilight. She tried to enjoy the view. When she drove with her father, she never got to ride shotgun—that seat was always for her mom,

A.J., or Nick. Still, tonight she wished she were in the back with Waverly.

The sounds of the marching band and the PA system grew louder, and Hannah bounced on her seat. She twisted her right earring, then the left one. This was the most important day of her brother's life so far, and she didn't want to miss it. She slammed the door behind her as soon as Dr. Wiggins pulled to the curb, then she sprinted toward the box office. Waverly and Libby could catch up. They seemed to be trying to ruin the night for her, but she wouldn't let them.

Lower Brynwood Memorial Stadium brimmed with noise and light, but not people. Too many losing seasons had dampened enthusiasm from the townspeople, so that only family members and the most bored high-schoolers bothered to show up. Hannah felt more nervous than before. The sparsely populated stadium was more intimidating than a full one. She could see each face, and what she saw wasn't cheerful.

Around the thirty-yard line, Hannah clambered up the aluminum bleachers. Waverly and Libby picked their way up the rickety metal steps behind her. Most other high schools in the area had spanking-new concrete stadiums, but at least the grass on the field was green. The assistant coach, Jake Laughlin, her brother's boss at the landscaping company, had donated field services, spraying enough chemicals to coax the rock-hard field into a patchwork of green, bright as artificial turf. Almost as bright as Martin's aunt's lawn.

"Where are you going?" Waverly demanded.

"You can see the game better from up high," Hannah said over her shoulder.

"But we can't see anyone from up there," Libby complained, trying to make eye contact with some boys who looked old enough to drive. The boys ignored her.

Hannah knew she meant that no one could see *them*. She preferred it that way. She caught a few people pointing and whispering at her. Everyone knew she was Nick's little sister—she looked like a football player with a ponytail. She took off the sparkly scarf and stuffed it in her pocket as she sat down, avoiding the mud on the seats from somebody else's footsteps.

She waved at her mom and dad, dressed in red and black, five rows back on the fifty-yard line. Her mom waved but didn't smile—too anxious, Hannah guessed. They all used to watch A.J. together as a family—Nick with his hair wet beneath a beanie, fresh from playing JV, and Hannah snuggling between her parents in a fleece blanket. Now she was old enough to sit with her friends, and A.J. perched a few rows behind them with his old high-school buddies, one of whom had a curly-haired baby, dressed in a Philadelphia Eagles jacket, on his knee. Even the babies knew better than to align themselves too closely with the Black Squirrels.

The band ran through "Louie, Louie," rather sloppily for a song played every game every year for the past four decades. They segued into "Hey Ya" as the flag-team girls pranced down the field in unitards, waving silk banners. Two held the ends of a paper banner painted with bubble letters spelling "Lo-B Rulz." Hannah was glad Martin wasn't there to see it.

The team was building up to its grand entrance—not so grand, actually, because the players had to jog the full distance from the gym lockers, through the parking lot, and over the soccer field. A.J. and Nick always complained about the lack of locker rooms in the stadium, and Hannah could see their point.

Hannah picked out Nick even without seeing his number—five, like Donovan McNabb had worn for the Eagles when they were kids. She smiled, just in case he could see her, too, but he seemed focused, staring straight ahead and bouncing from foot to foot. Waverly and Libby were still chatting.

A drumroll rattled and the loudspeaker boomed, "Ladies and gentleman, the Black Squirrels!" Hannah yelled so loud she didn't care if anyone else made a noise.

Nick burst through the paper banner, the rest of the team flowing behind him like a red and black cattle drive. Head Coach Schmidt brought up the rear, his ball cap so high on his head it looked like it might pop off if he took a deep breath. His red nylon pullover was big enough to land a paratrooper and stretched tight over his gut. It was a stark contrast to Assistant Coach Laughlin, beefy but trim in a black polo and sharply peaked cap.

Lower Brynwood won the coin toss, and the offensive line set up at the twenty-yard line after the kickoff ended in a touchback. Nick took the snap and dropped out of the pocket. He sent a low spiral to Chase, who shook off a defender to pull in the ball at the thirty-five. He spun to avoid a tackle and took off, accelerating toward the forty-five, the forty, the thirty-five. Even Waverly and Libby leaped to their feet. One defensive back and thirty yards of grass lay between Chase and the first touchdown of the season. He stutter-stepped, and his knee crumpled beneath him on the hard turf. Even from a distance Hannah heard the solid *thwack* of flesh against plastic against flesh. She wasn't sure if the grunt came before the hit or after, but then the groan turned to a wail.

The spectators fell silent. The wail grew louder. Defenders peeled off, and she could see Chase sprawled on the field, clutching his leg and twisting in pain. He was Nick's best receiver, down after the first play.

The trainers jogged out, Coach Schmidt following, his belly and neck rolls bouncing with each step. A circle of players formed around the outer ring of trainers. After a few minutes, Chase emerged from the wall of shoulder pads, hobbling under his own power, a trainer and the assistant coach each with an arm around him as they escorted him to the sidelines. After a few moments bending over Chase's leg as the player's face contorted in agony, a trainer called over the ambulance, standing by as always on the side of the field. The EMTs shuffled Chase into the back, silently turned on the lights, and rolled out of the parking lot.

"Whoa," said Libby. "Bad luck."

Bad luck, Hannah thought. The team had enough bad luck already. Injuries happened on athletic fields every day, but she couldn't help thinking of the curse. Hannah stared at the field. In the middle of the once-immaculate green was a scorched brown patch, the size and shape of a body. The grass was dead where Chase had lain writhing in agony. Burnt dry.

She caught a flare of light in the corner of her eye. High above the end zone, sparks sprayed from the ancient electronic scoreboard. One light bulb shattered in a blaze of fire and a spray of glass, then another, then all the lights blazed on and faded slowly. The scoreboard went dark. Broken down and worn out, like everything else in Lower Brynwood.

After a few minutes, the grounds crew wheeled out a portable scoreboard and the teams resumed play, but Nick had nowhere to throw.

The Black Squirrels lost, twenty-eight to ten.

13

The Yearbook

The cursor blinked, and Martin waited. In a hot, dry room on the other side of the world, his mother was typing.

HOW'S SCHOOL?

COOL. I ALREADY LEARNED WHAT THEY'RE DOING IN MATH. He drummed his fingers while he waited.

I MEANT HOW DO YOU LIKE THE KIDS? WHAT ABOUT THAT KID YOU MENTIONED MEETING THE OTHER DAY? STILL HANGING OUT WITH HIM?

SHE'S ACTUALLY A GIRL — HANNAH. WE'RE WORKING ON A COMMUNITY SERVICE PROJECT 2GETHER.

INTERESTING.

NOT REALLY.

WE'LL SEE. WHAT ABOUT SPORTS? MAYBE X COUNTRY?

NO TEAM FOR KIDS MY AGE. BUT I'M JOINING A NEW CLUB. JUNIOR JUNIOR EXECUTIVES OF TOMORROW. As he waited for a response, the doorbell rang.

HA! THAT DOESN'T SOUND LIKE YOU.

IT'S AUNT MICHELLE'S IDEA.

He listened to his aunt open the door and cheerily address whoever stood there.

"What are you selling, sweetie?" she said. Martin couldn't hear an answer.

THAT SOUNDS LIKE SOMETHING MICHELLE WOULD LIKE, Martin's mother typed. He snickered, picturing her rolling her eyes like she always did when she talked about Aunt Michelle. Then Aunt Michelle's voice chased the image of his mother from his head.

"Then do you have a petition you want me to sign?" Aunt Michelle said in her fakest sweet voice to the person at the door.

SHE THINKS BUSINESS TRAINING WOULD HELP ME FOCUS, Martin typed.

"Martin? Yes, he's here." He heard Aunt Michelle's high heels clacking toward the room.

FOCUS IS THE LAST THING YOU NEED. BUT MAYBE YOU'LL MEET MORE NICE KIDS LIKE THAT HANNAH, his mom typed. She was always nagging him to meet new people, spend time on something other than video games.

The footsteps came closer. Was it one person or two? He hurriedly typed, GOT TO GO, MOM. I LOVE YOU.

I LOVE YOU TOO. VIDEO CHAT YOU TOMORROW, IF IT'S WORKING.

SAME BAT TIME.

SAME BAT CHANNEL, his mom typed, and then her icon went dark.

Aunt Michelle's footsteps stopped at the door and she peered in without knocking. Martin clicked the window shut to keep her from reading over his shoulder. His mother's words disappeared into the ether, and a sharp pang stabbed him in his chest. IM conversations were nothing like the real thing. And Aunt Michelle was nothing like his mother.

"There's a girl to see you, Martin," said Aunt Michelle. "See, that positive thinking has worked already. All you have to do is sit there and the girls flock to your door."

Martin spun the chair around to glare at her. "Hannah's just a friend. We're doing a project together."

"For now," Aunt Michelle said, half-winking at him. "Keep your mind on what you want, and you get it."

"Alrighty." Anything to stop the mantras. "If Hannah's here, I have to go now."

"Fine. Be back in time to rake the leaves."

He closed the door behind him as quick as he could. Hannah stood on the step. Not a leaf was in sight. *What leaves?* he thought.

"So, did your brother win?" Martin asked.

"They lost," Hannah said, sounding almost accusing.

"What else is new?" He sniffed.

"It's worse than that. Chase, the guy with the knife at the tree, tore his ACL."

"His what?"

"ACL—anterior cruciate ligament. It's one of the four ligaments of the knee, often injured during lateral movements," Hannah said, sounding like a TV doctor. He wondered if she had rehearsed. "He's out for the season—maybe for good."

"So?" Martin didn't care except that he knew it mattered to her.

"He's the best receiver Lower Brynwood has! Maybe you don't care, but Nick doesn't have a chance at a scholarship if there's no one to catch the ball."

"I'm sorry about your brother, but that guy—Chase—had it coming." His empathy only extended so far.

"Maybe. But what really matters is that the curse is getting worse. The team didn't just lose—the scoreboard exploded!"

"Really?" Martin perked up. "It exploded?"

"Well, it burned out. But the timing was weird, and the broken glass could have cut someone. And the grass died!

It was just like the tree. And Chase is really hurt—anybody could be next."

Martin thought of his mom and reassured himself that a curse couldn't reach her in Afghanistan. But did he really know how curses worked? Did he want to find out? "So, what do we do?"

She held up an ancient-looking book. "There's something you have to see."

14

The Witch's House

"I'm beginning to feel like your trainer," Hannah said as she pedaled alongside Martin.

"Then you ought to go faster," he said. "You're too easy on me."

"Maybe next time." She hit the brakes with a screech and hopped off her bike. "We're here." They stood in front of Jenna Blitzer's cottage, Martin trying to stay upright until his jellied limbs solidified again.

"Cottage" wasn't quite the right word, Martin realized. Like a miniature castle transplanted from an Arlithean mountainside, this house was vertical, not low to the ground—three stories, a sharply pitched roof, and such a small footprint that there couldn't have been more than one or two rooms per floor. The complicated geometry of the many-gabled roof was repeated in three painted, peaked-roof wood hutches that stood in the garden like windowless dollhouses. Smaller houses hung from the trees and perched on metal posts. *Like heads on pikes*, he thought grimly. A warning against trespassers.

"Did that mysterious book of yours tell you to come here?" Martin said.

"Sort of. It's the key to the mystery."

"What is it? Some kind of magic text?" he said. Hannah propped up her bike on the kickstand and pulled the book out of her bag, holding it up with a flourish.

It was just an old yearbook. He raised an eyebrow.

"This is important, Martin," she said. "Look! It belongs to Dr. Wiggins—1989, just like the oldest carving. And look at this." Hannah turned to a black and white page filled with grainy group shots. "And this!" She pulled the notebook out of her bag and flipped it open. Martin took the book from her. All he saw was a bunch of kids in ugly clothes and bad haircuts, but Hannah acted like the book held some big revelation. "See?" she said, triumphant. "EEEEEE. That carving isn't an eye chart. It's an acronym."

"You mean an abbreviation. An acronym is initials that spell a word."

"Whatever! It stands for this club—Environment, Ecology, and Energy Efficiency for an Enlightened Earth."

"Maybe." Martin had to admit the coincidence was strange, and there was nothing he loved as much as strange coincidences.

"Look! See who's the president?" She jabbed at the page.

"Jenna Blitzer? You're saying she's the witch?" He had thought that anyone who tweaked Aunt Michelle couldn't be bad, but now he wasn't so sure. Was Jenna the bad one? He peered at the little house and its small miniatures among the greenery. It looked as if the cottage was reproducing itself. He couldn't decide if it was creepy, or what his mom would call charming. He shivered as the sweat evaporated from his skin. Definitely creepy.

"I don't like that word, 'witch.' It sounds sexist. But maybe she's the bad one," Hannah said, shaking her ponytail. "Look what's printed on her T-shirt."

"Tree-hugger."

"It's almost a confession. Remember what we said—the curse was probably set by someone looking for revenge or personal gain. And if Jenna knew anybody was carving up a tree, she'd definitely want revenge."

"Back it up," Martin said. "Let's think about this. Wouldn't that mean she carved the six Es to do it? Does that make sense, that she would hurt the tree to save the tree?"

"Maybe. Obsessed people will go to crazy lengths. You've heard of ecoterrorism, right? Super-extreme environmentalists burn down housing developments and shopping malls to save nature. Cutting a symbol into a tree is a lot less drastic, isn't it?"

"Good point. But don't we need a plan before we approach her?" This was going too fast. Martin and Gord had spent half the summer planning a raid on an Arlithean stronghold, and it would have gone perfectly if Martin hadn't moved to Lower Brynwood first.

"We have a suspect, a plan, and a cover story. All we have to do is knock on Jenna's door and we can ask all the questions we want. If we say we're trying to save the Spirit Tree for a school project, she'll be eating out of our hands."

As long as she doesn't bite them off, Martin thought. "Shouldn't we rehearse what we're going to say?"

"Just follow my lead. As far as she knows, we're just dumb kids—she won't expect us to know what we're talking about."

The gravel path crunched under their feet, loud as an alarm. There was no bell or knocker on the arched oak door—just a lighter area where the knocker must have been once. Hannah rapped her knuckles against the wood. They waited a moment, and Martin tried to think of something clever to say. No one answered.

Martin pounded with the side of his fist. Nothing.

"After all that, nobody's home," Martin said, unclenching his hands.

"We came all this way. We might as well look in the windows," Hannah said.

Martin rubbed his head, tousling his damp hair so that it stood up more wildly than before. "I don't know."

"How about we walk around to the back door?" Hannah suggested, as if she was coaxing a baby to take his first steps. "If we happen to see in the windows at the same time, it's not our fault."

The small casement windows were above eye level and shuttered, yielding no views into the dark house. Hannah and Martin climbed onto a small covered back porch furnished with a hanging wooden swing and cluttered with an assortment of bright rubber clogs and muddy, mismatched garden tools—unlike Aunt Michelle's perfect set, these tools had definitely been used, Martin noted. Hannah knocked at the dented aluminum storm door. Nothing.

"That was useless," Martin said. "Let's come back tomorrow with a better plan in place."

Ignoring him, Hannah craned her neck and jumped up, trying to peek over the shutters. "Maybe we can see inside if we stand on one of those little tool sheds."

"Hannah, you said we would just knock."

"We did. But we didn't learn anything yet. No one will see us from the street." She walked over to the nearest red-painted box and looked for a foothold.

Martin sighed. Hannah was going to keep going, no matter what he said. "Let me do it," he said. "I'm lighter than you are." She frowned as he scrambled up the hardware on the side of the box. He lost his balance for a moment as he straightened, clomping heavily with one foot on either side of the peaked roof. "I can't see anything."

"Uh, Martin?" Hannah said with the kind of calm that hid fear.

"What now?"

"I don't think that's a tool shed you're standing on."

The insect buzz in the garden had gotten louder. Martin realized it was coming from the wooden box beneath his feet. A line of angry bees looped from the underside of what he now realized was a giant beehive.

"You'd better get down from there," Hannah said. "Slowly."

Too late. He leaped off, clearing the hive by a good eight feet, but the cloud of bees followed. He dropped to the ground and waved them off his head and face, blinded with pain as if he'd been shot with a hundred flaming arrows.

"Children!" The cry came from the back porch, but Martin was still curled up. A tall woman came streaming toward him and lifted him up. All the bees were gone, except for the dead and dying clinging to the stingers embedded in his arms.

"You're not allergic, are you, son?" the woman said, peering into his eyes with nearly lashless blue ones. Her wet hair dripped, leaving damp spots on the shoulders of her fuzzy fleece pullover.

"No, ma'am. I don't think so." His arms and face felt like they were burning.

"Good." Jenna held up each of his arms, seeming to silently count the welts. "Come onto the porch and I'll take care of those stings."

Martin obeyed, but Hannah lingered behind, looking as if she was about to take off running. "You come, too, miss. I'll get you both a drink while we wait for your parents to pick you up."

"My parents?"

"I can't let you walk home, just in case something happens. Lucky for you I was home. I thought I heard a knock but by the time I got out of the shower you were already screaming.""

Martin was in too much pain to resist. He let Jenna steer him, settling him onto the porch swing. At least his butt hadn't been stung. Hannah lagged, waiting until the door slammed behind Jenna before approaching sideways, her nose and mouth screwed up in apology. Her weight on the porch swing set it to creaking.

"Are you okay? You don't look so good," she said, somehow gazing into his eyes without quite making eye contact. He realized she was looking at his pupils, probably trying to gauge whether he was about to pass out.

"I don't feel so good. Why did you make me stand on a beehive?"

"I didn't know what it was! It seemed like a good idea at the time."

It didn't seem like a good idea to me, Martin thought. Follow my lead, she'd said, and he had. Like she had him hypnotized. He said aloud, "Maybe it was the curse."

"You could have been killed."

"The day's not over. There's plenty of time for me to get killed after I call Aunt Michelle and she finds out I'm consorting with her worst enemy. Can I borrow your cell phone?" he asked.

She shook her head. "Mine doesn't work right now. Disconnected until the first of the month. But we can't call your aunt, anyway. She'll ask questions."

"I'm more worried about Jenna. She won't tell us anything if she finds out I'm related to Michelle Medina, Brynwood Estates Community Association President. She'll think I was spying on her."

"We *were* spying on her," Hannah said.

"Maybe. But not about her lawn."

"Then we'd better learn everything we can, as soon as we can. I'll call your aunt. You try to find out if she's the one who cursed the tree."

Jenna opened the door, and Hannah and Martin leaned as far away from each other as possible. Jenna balanced two glasses of iced tea on an aluminum first-aid kit. "Let's get you taken care of, shall we?"

She handed out the drinks and opened the kit. "You ought to take an oral antihistamine, just in case you have an allergic reaction. I don't want to give it to you without permission from your parents. Could you call them?"

"My mom's in Afghanistan and my dad's in Florida," Martin said. He realized that sounded whiny, but he couldn't help wishing his mom was there. The pain ran up and down his arm like the fire had in the tree, flaring up in a sharp point of agony at each welt. "I'll have to call my aunt."

"Go ahead.

"Neither of us have cell phones that work."

"You must be the last two holdouts on the planet, besides me," Jenna said. The shiny skin around her eyes crinkled when she smiled. "The phone's on the wall in the kitchen, opposite the door."

Hannah hopped up. "I'll take care of it." She scribbled the phone number from Martin's notebook onto her hand, then gave it back, pointing at the notebook and pen with her raised eyebrows. "You take care of Martin, Ms. Blitzer." She slammed the door behind her, and Jenna opened the bottle of calamine lotion.

"So, you know my name," she said, dabbing a cotton ball onto the swollen lumps on his skin. "And now I know yours, Martin. Who's your friend?"

"That's Hannah." He winced, then steeled himself. His whole body hurt and he couldn't think straight. He knew Hannah wanted him to ask questions, but he had an uneasy feeling he was going to be the one answering them.

"What exactly were you two doing to my beehive? There are better ways to get honey. There's some in that iced tea—no theft required."

"We didn't know it was a hive. We were just looking for you. We're working on a seventh-grade local history project, and we thought you would be a good person to ask."

"I'm not a historian. But I do believe in preservation," she said, indicating her antique cottage with a little nod of her head. "What's the project?"

"We're trying to preserve all the messages on the Spirit Tree—you know, that big old tree in the park with all the carvings—and find out the history behind it."

"The Spirit Tree?" Jenna said, fixing him with her penetrating pale eyes. "The history in that tree has nothing to do with what's carved on it."

He nodded. "We know it was there during the Revolutionary War, and when the mill was built, when it closed, all that."

"That's not what I mean. That's *human* history. Plants have a history of their own. To a tree, we're like mayflies buzzing through its leaves. Here one minute, gone in an instant. Its history is written inside."

"You mean, like the rings on a tree?" Martin said, touching one of the hard, hot welts on his arm. It reminded him of the scarred bark around the carved words on the tree. Was this how the tree felt? "We can't see those unless we cut it down."

"Don't scratch," she said, gently pushing his hand away and dabbing at the wound. "I didn't mean the rings. The history is deeper. It's invisible to the naked eye. The language it's written in isn't yet fully understood by science. By humans."

"Language?" Martin thought of how the tree had spoken to them—the words flashing fire in the bark. She couldn't mean that—could she?

"We call it language, but that's just a metaphor. Humans speak in language, but for plants, history is written in a more elemental way." She capped the bottle and set it on a wobbly cast-iron table.

"The language of trees? Sounds like something from a fantasy—like magic," Martin said.

She shook her head. "Magic is another metaphor used to make sense of natural phenomena people don't understand. You could call it a spell, a recipe, a formula, or a code. History is written in the tree's cells. It's in the DNA of the fruit it drops every fall. It's in the chemical and electrical signals it sends through the soil and in the air."

Martin's skin tingled, adding to the pain. "Signals?"

"In a way. Plants have evolved complex signals to communicate under stress, or to entice pollinators. Not just your friends the bees, but butterflies, carrion flies, even frogs and bats."

"You're saying plants can talk." Dryads, wild sylvans—trees that spoke and moved. All those myths had to come from somewhere.

Her laugh was surprisingly girlish. "Nothing of the sort. The idea that plants are sentient is science fiction, not science. Paranormal research. But I know a little about it—maybe because I wish that it were true. It's documented that plants have electromagnetic properties and respond to stimuli. Does that mean they feel pleasure and pain? That they think and feel? It's not possible—they don't have limbic systems. Sometimes I talk to my plants, but the plain truth is that they can't talk back. They can't even hear me."

Hannah came through the door. *Bad timing*, Martin thought. This conversation was finally going somewhere.

"Martin's aunt said it's okay to give him the medicine," Hannah said. "But she's too busy at work to pick him up. My brother's coming to get us."

The fire in Martin's arm cooled slightly as the lotion began to work. He swallowed the antihistamine capsule with a gulp of honey tea. "Hair of the dog that bit you," his mom would say after a late night with her friends.

Hannah spoke again. "So, did Martin tell you we were trying to save the tree?"

"Save the tree?" Jenna asked, an edge coming into her voice, and Martin could feel her teetering back into distrust. "Save it from what? Martin just mentioned that you were working on a history project."

"That's how we started out—trying to figure out what the carvings meant. But the tree looks sick. We think it might be dying."

Jenna drilled Martin with a hard look. "He didn't mention that, either."

"Well, we wrote down some of the messages, and we wondered if you could help us figure out what they mean."

"I don't care what the messages say. It's the tree that would interest me."

"Us, too! That's what we were hoping you'd say," Hannah said, nudging Martin. He wished she would be more subtle. He could tell Jenna wasn't missing a single gesture or look that passed between them. "We thought the messages would tell us when it all started and how to stop it."

"If you want to know how to stop the disease, I'm not the right person. I'm not a horticulturalist," Jenna said. "But maybe one of my colleagues could help."

"Colleagues?" Hannah asked.

"Didn't you come to me because I'm a landscape ecologist at the university center for sustainable development? I often work with the extension office."

Martin had no idea what any of that meant, but he knew better than to ask or risk blowing whatever credibility they had. Not only was Jenna buying their cover, more or less, she might be able to help if they played this right. Hannah knit her straight eyebrows and opened her mouth as if another question was about to tumble out.

A loud honk made them all jump.

"There's my brother," Hannah said. "We'd better get going. We're really, really sorry we disturbed your bees. Can we come back and talk more when Martin's feeling better?"

Jenna nodded, drawing a hand through her wet ringlets as she glanced over at A.J.'s truck. "Next time I'll try to be more presentable if you try not to injure yourselves again. I can ask a few questions at the university, but I can't promise anything."

"Thanks, Ms. Blitzer." Martin put out his hand, regretting it when pain vibrated up his arm as she gently grasped his fingers and shook.

"That's *Dr.* Blitzer, Martin. But you can both call me Jenna."

15

Painted Lady

Hannah had a hard time looking Martin in the eye now that she had nearly killed him. The angry red welt on the middle of his forehead and the one on his cheek didn't help, either.

She took a last look at Jenna's wild garden through the car window. How had she ever thought it was decrepit? It was one of the most beautiful places in Lower Brynwood— the most *alive*. Jenna was still watching them, but Hannah couldn't tell if she looked suspicious or thoughtful. She stretched across Martin to wave at Jenna, who waved back half-heartedly with her crossed arms.

Martin leaned against the door as if he didn't want to touch her. She didn't blame him, but she worried the lock on the door wouldn't hold against his weight. The truck rattled, and with every bump she pictured him falling out into the street.

"Did you find out anything about the curse?" she asked in a low voice, leaning into Martin so A.J. wouldn't hear. Her brother was listening to sports radio, volume turned up too loud, and she knew he'd rather not be interrupted by anything Hannah and Martin said anyway.

"It didn't come up," Martin said, fingering the swollen bumps on his arm.

"Then what were you talking about? She said she was a doctor, but it sounded like some kind of new-age thing." Kind of witchy, actually, if Hannah was honest, but she wouldn't admit it. She always meant to be a doctor or scientist, but she had never expected a scientist to be quite like Jenna.

"So she's a new-age doctor—sustainability and ecology and all that. A landscape ecologist, whatever that is."

"That's even better," Hannah said. "She could really help us."

"Don't tell me that you changed your mind about whether Jenna is a suspect."

"No," Hannah said, trailing off. She might have jumped to conclusions about Jenna too quickly, but she wouldn't admit it yet. The truck wound through the subdivision, passing stucco houses dominated by double garages facing the street. "She's the best lead we have, but that could mean she's a source, not a suspect. If Jenna's a scientist, she couldn't be all bad."

"Haven't you ever heard of an evil scientist?" Martin said. "Or one of those eco-terrorist types you were talking about earlier?"

"Okay, we keep an eye on her. She definitely has a lot to tell us, if we can get it out of her," Hannah said. The houses here were a lot bigger and newer than in her neighborhood, but most of the lawns were just as brown and weedy. It was still Lower Brynwood, despite the fancy name. "Hey, your aunt said she was vice-president of Horizon Network Communications when she answered my call. Can't you get a cell phone from her?"

"I could if I had sixty bucks a month to pay for a plan, same as you. Aunt Michelle doesn't give anything away. Hey

A.J., this is close enough," Martin said, raising his voice as the truck reached the corner of his aunt's cul-de-sac.

"You sure?" A.J. asked. He peered up the block toward the one bright green lawn.

"I'd rather walk up to the house, if you know what I mean," Martin said. "Fewer questions."

"Suits me," A.J. said, pulling to the curb. "Just in case your aunt has some emergency lawn care she wants done off the clock."

When Martin got out of the truck, Hannah leaned her forehead against the window. She twisted the earring in her right ear, remembering when she had met Jenna before.

A few years earlier, she and Waverly had decided to dress as butterflies for Halloween. Hannah made her own costume, copying a pattern from her Girl Scout handbook, creating a small pattern on a grid and then enlarging it onto poster board. Her mother helped make a shoulder harness and handholds. The wings didn't stick up that well by themselves, but she could flap them.

She had been proud until she saw the costume Waverly had ordered from an online costume shop. Waverly's wings were gauzy pink, dripping with glitter and rhinestones, and her eyelids and cheekbones gleamed with silver and purple swirls. She even wore frosty pink lip gloss, all the better for simpering at A.J., who had agreed to take the two of them trick-or-treating. He was too old to go by himself, but he could collect his own haul if he put on a hobo outfit and accompanied two little girls.

"Oh, a monarch butterfly and a fairy princess!" the first old lady had said when they held out their plastic pumpkins. Hannah tried to tell the first woman that she was a painted lady, the kind of butterfly she had raised from caterpillars every spring since she was five years old. The woman gave her a shocked look, as if she was some other kind of painted lady. The woman at the next house just looked confused, so Hannah stopped correcting them. A.J. told her she'd get more candy that way, and he knew what he was talking about.

A.J. was the perfect chaperone—old enough to make them feel safe, and young enough to enjoy scaring them silly. No matter how many times he jumped out at them, Waverly and Hannah screamed. But at the witch's house they all paused. Most children avoided the spooky stone cottage, which didn't need holiday decorations to look a hundred times more haunted than the tract homes with cobweb-draped graveyards in the front lawn. A.J. let out a loud *whooooo*, working Waverly and Hannah into a frenzy of half-pretend fear, and they clutched his hands as they followed the solar lights on the path to knock on the heavy arched door.

The blue-eyed woman who opened it didn't look like a witch. She recognized Hannah as a painted lady butterfly right away, exclaiming over the homemade costume. She gave each child a full-sized Nestle Crunch—rare generosity in the neighborhood.

Hannah had been more thrilled with Jenna's comments than the candy.

Hannah had known then that Jenna wasn't a witch. A witch would give out poisoned apples, or maybe ancient Starlight Mints that tasted like mothballs—kind of like the ones that first old lady had given them. Witches didn't hand out full-sized candy bars, at least not in Lower Brynwood.

Sitting in the cab of A.J.'s truck, Hannah wondered if he remembered that night, too. She switched off the radio.

"Hey, I was listening to that!" A.J. reached for the button. "This was a tough day—you wouldn't believe the number of downed trees. I had to clear a whole street full of Bradford pears that toppled like dominoes. Looked like a tornado hit them."

Hannah frowned sympathetically, but she didn't take her hand away from the radio controls. "I'll put the radio back on if you swear you won't tell."

"Tell what?"

"Any of it. Not about Jenna and the bee stings. If Mom hears what happened to Martin, she's going to call Michelle Medina to see how he is, and the gig's up."

"What gig?"

"I don't know. Whatever a gig is."

A.J. nodded. "I guess you covered for me often enough when I came in late after a party or a date. I don't mind covering for you about the tree—as long as that's all it is. You don't really *like* that kid, do you?"

"No way! Not like that." Hannah's face blazed hot, and then she felt guilty for saying it. She didn't want anyone to think he was her boyfriend, but Martin was okay. "I mean, I do like him as a friend. And I feel bad for him—his mom's in Afghanistan, and he's stuck here with Madame President Medina. I just know that if she finds out Martin is doing, well, *anything*, she's sure to stop it."

"Especially if she knew it was about a tree. From what I've seen of her, she'd clear-cut the whole woods if it kept a single leaf off her lawn," A.J. snorted.

"And she already hates Jenna. Which reminds me—do you know what the university extension office is?"

"Sure. It's a branch of the college of agricultural sciences. They run classes for gardeners, farmers, and even lowly landscapers like me. I wanted to take some classes to get certified as an arborist, but Bossman Jake said I'd be better off learning from him. Why?"

"Jenna works for them." Hannah remembered what A.J. had said about the fallen Bradford pears. "Last night was really clear and still, wasn't it?"

"I guess."

"Why do you think those trees fell over?"

"I don't know. Those stupid things keel over if you look at them funny. Or maybe they got whatever blight's bothering that Spirit Tree of yours. It's getting harder and harder to keep anything alive here." A.J. broke off as he pulled into the alley behind the Vaughan house. A shiny red SUV blocked the driveway. He let out a curse. "That's Jake's truck," he said. "Bossman just *had* to show up after the day I had."

By the time A.J. found a street parking spot and he and Hannah hauled themselves two blocks to the house, Jake Laughlin was already leaving.

"Jake," said A.J., sounding more enthusiastic than Hannah knew he was. "What can I do for you?"

"Nothing at all." Jake laughed uncomfortably, raking a hand through his spiky reddish-brown hair. "I came to see your little brother. Well, not so little anymore."

A.J.'s jaw tightened, and Hannah guessed that the emotion he was hiding now was disappointment. Even if he hated Jake, Hannah knew it hurt knowing that Nick was the one everyone wanted these days. "Of course. You're the assistant football coach," he said.

Jake patted a leather bag and then hurled it into the passenger seat. "New playbooks for the offense. With Chase out of commission, we're going to have to work our superstar quarterback harder."

A.J. smiled, but he looked smaller since his boss had shown up. "Nick won't let you down."

"Of course he won't. If he can dream it, he can be it. Just like I don't plan on being assistant coach forever. Take a lesson, A.J. You won't get to lead one of my landscaping crews until you put your mind to it."

A.J. looked as if he was about to say something he might regret, so Hannah jumped in. "Mr. Laughlin? Could I ask you something?"

He looked at her for the first time.

"You know the Spirit Tree? The old carved-up tree in the woods?"

He nodded, and she thought about gazing beseechingly at him through her lashes the way Waverly always practiced in the mirror. Ugh. His head was the size of a bulldog's but not nearly as cute. Forget it—she couldn't act like Waverly, but she had to convince him her own way. "It looks a little sick. A.J. came out to look at it, but he couldn't tell what was wrong." She ignored A.J. glaring at her and said, "We thought you'd know since you're the expert."

"Look, Hannah, I probably could take care of it, but I don't have a contract with the township for the work. Laughlin Landscaping and Tree Care is a business, and money doesn't grow on trees."

"But if you're a tree surgeon, it kind of does, doesn't it?" Hannah said. Jake looked at her, not sure how to react. Hannah forced herself to giggle, then A.J. managed to cough out a laugh, and finally Jake joined in.

"Nobody gets rich working for free, little girl."

"You can if you get publicity for doing it. A friend and I are studying the tree for a town history project. If we let the *Lower Brynwood Weekly Herald* know you're helping, I bet they'd do a story on it. They'd let everybody know that Laughlin Landscaping does more than cut lawns—you're tree-care professionals. And you're a community leader! You'd get lots of new business."

"Your little sister has a point." Jake turned to A.J. "You can't buy good will, but it's the most precious thing you own. You could take a lesson from her, too, A.J."

Hannah shrugged behind Jake's back in apology. His boss sure was an idiot. This wasn't how she meant the day to end for her brother, especially after he'd helped her. But Jake agreed to look at the tree during the week. Hopefully he was better with plants than he was with human beings.

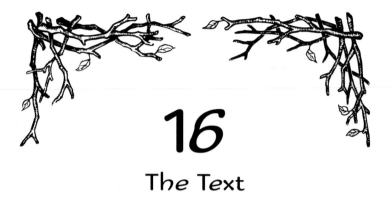

16

The Text

Hannah walked in the woods at night.

The moon reflected off the bark of the saplings, but it was too bright, too silver. She realized the trees were dead, the bare wood bleached smooth and white—the bones of a forest still standing, petrified like fossils. Dead wood.

A cloud passed over the moon, although the sky had been clear and starry a moment before.

A burst of lightning split the darkness, and Hannah felt electricity around her, lifting the hair from her head and the golden down from her arms. For a moment she thought the energy would lift her as well, but then something began pulling at her feet. She tried to walk, but she felt rooted— no, that wasn't the right word. Her feet weren't growing into the earth—they were being dragged down, scraping through grit and silt. The electricity tore at her hair, the tension tugging up and outward, the ground sucking her downward, her body stretched between.

She woke feeling drained and empty. Was that how the tree felt?

Scritch scratch. She knew it was just the sound of branches on the roof, but the thought didn't comfort her. It was a long time before she fell asleep again.

The next morning Hannah couldn't close her bag. Her giant textbooks alone took up too much room, and the Lower Brynwood yearbook was the last straw. She considered leaving it at home, but instead took out her social studies book and balanced it in the wire basket on the front of the bike. Only when she was bungee-cording her messenger bag onto the back rack did she realize why the bike seemed extra awkward when she dragged it up the stairs. The rear tire was flat.

She swore silently. Her luck was getting worse. She pulled her cell phone from a zipped pocket. At least the clock still worked, even if she couldn't get calls. She swore aloud now. Late, late, late. She could catch the bus if she left now, but she wouldn't have time to go inside to tell Waverly she wasn't coming.

She jumped when her phone pinged. No way. She still was out of airtime.

New message. She clicked it open.

One word: HURRY.

The bus rounded the corner, taking the turn wide. Hurry!

Hannah swore louder. She swung her bag over one shoulder and ran, the heavy books bruising her hip with each step. If she didn't get to the stop in time, the bus driver wouldn't slow down.

Only when she had flopped in an empty seat did she begin to think clearly.

Hannah always carried the phone because it had a clock and her phone book, but she shouldn't be able to get messages until her parents recharged her crummy pay-as-you-go plan with more minutes at the beginning of the month. So who had texted her? She read the message again.

HURRY.

No number listed. She scanned the faces of the kids on the bus. Half-asleep or deep in conversation, none of them looked up. None of them would have warned her that the bus was coming, anyway.

Hannah dialed Waverly, hoping her phone airtime had been replenished by her parents, or some other miracle. Nothing. She banged her forehead on the window. When she saw the flat tire, she should have just gone inside and called Waverly. Dr. Wiggins would have picked her up. They were probably still waiting for her, and she had no way to reach them with her cell phone out of operation. She wouldn't even be able to explain to Waverly until after social studies. If Waverly would even listen then.

Social studies! She had left her textbook strapped on the bike, and her homework was folded inside. She had never missed an assignment—not once. She wasn't even at school yet and this was already the worst day ever.

Her phone pinged again. This time she hesitated, but she had to see what the text said.

HURRY. TIME IS RUNNING OUT.

17

The Spirit Tree

The tree was patient. When it needed water or sun, it waited. When winter came, it slept. Humans crowded it once, and then they faltered and disappeared.

A season to a tree is like a day to a human. A year is like a week.

But the tree was crumbling, drained from the inside. A desiccated shell.

The tree would not live to see another season or another year.

The time for patience was over.

18

Pretending to Be a Chair

Martin knew what it looked like to avoid being called on, because he'd been practicing ever since he came to this miserable town. So when Hannah slumped down in her seat, Martin could tell that whatever kind of bad morning she'd had was about to get worse. Because Mr. Michaelson knew that pretending-to-be-a-chair strategy better than Martin did. And today was the day he decided to call on Hannah.

Every other day Martin had seen Hannah wave her arm so wildly it looked like she was raising the social studies roof. Usually Mr. Michaelson ignored her unless hers was the only hand in the air. Martin knew teachers called it "giving someone else a chance," but sometimes he thought the most popular teachers secretly despised the smart kids. Those teachers had probably laughed at that kind of kid back when they were C-plus starters on the baseball team or president of the Spirit Club or whatever. They had had all the power then, and as faculty, they still had power—a grade book and a teacher's guide with the answers printed in bright red ink. They weren't about to let those know-it-all nerds get one over on them.

Mr. Michaelson didn't seem like that type of teacher, though. He liked the nerds. He tried to look hip with his dark shirts, matching ties and rimless glasses, but Martin could tell that, ten years ago, he probably wore a fanny pack to hold his graphing calculator and twenty-sided die. If he were a kid today, he'd be building his own computer and subscribing to the multiplayer online RPG of *Dragon Era*, just like Martin. Heck, Mr. Michaelson probably did that, anyway. He might drive a crap car, but he could buy a mighty fine gaming system if he wanted to.

Anyway, he was one of Martin's people.

Today that meant he wasn't one of Hannah's. Because Hannah wasn't just a smart kid. Today she wore a red and black soccer jersey, satiny piped shorts, matching sneakers and one of those stretchy things girls put on their ponytails. Today she was clearly a star of the soccer team, bedecked in full game-day regalia for lesser mortals to admire.

"I've heard some grumbles about the amount of last night's homework. Ms. Vaughan," Mr. Michaelson said, giving her last name two syllables. Hannah unpeeled her head from the desk, "Could you read off your answer to question number one?"

"No." She turned as red as her jersey. "I mean, I did the homework, but I don't have it. I got a flat tire and I forgot it."

"Surely you remember what you wrote—the instigating factors in the Whiskey Rebellion. It might help if you cracked open your textbook."

"I don't have my book, either." She slumped down a little further.

"I see. You managed to remember your uniform, but not your school work," Mr. Michaelson said, narrowing his eyes. "Next time don't forget which word comes first in 'student-athlete.'"

Hannah mumbled an apology.

"You can share Libby's book. I'm sure she won't mind."

Libby smirked at Hannah, who scooched over, but somehow Libby kept blocking the text whenever she tossed her glossy curtain of hair. A week earlier, Martin would have been glad to see Hannah humiliated in social studies. But not anymore.

Mr. Michaelson asked another question, but Hannah didn't raise her hand. No one else did, either. Martin knew the answer, but he just stared stonily ahead, letting the teacher twist in the wind, waiting for a response that never came.

Later at lunch Martin should have been getting a jump on homework while he ate, but instead he mentally replayed one of his favorite confrontations—the battle between the ranger and the Arlithean hordes after they had kidnapped the Worlinzer sorceress, Lady Torthea.

Thus, he was less prepared than usual when Hannah plopped down next him. He glanced over at her usual spot, where Waverly huddled with Libby. Behind the two girls, a cafeteria table was lined shoulder to shoulder with red and black jerseys, each with a different shade and texture of ponytail flowing down the back.

"To what do I owe the pleasure, my lady?" he said in a low tone.

"What?" she said, eying the exits as if about to flee.

Martin cleared his throat, pretending to cough. Then he said in his normal voice, "What's up?"

"Nothing good. The curse is getting worse. Take a look at this."

Hannah handed him her phone. He held it up, trying to block the glare from the fluorescent lights.

"Be careful. If Mr. Michaelson sees it, he'll confiscate it for sure. No phones during the school day."

"Sorry." He held it under the folding table.

HURRY. TIME IS RUNNING OUT.

He lifted his eyebrows. "What? Is a shoe sale almost over at Brynwood Park Mall? This is worse luck than me getting attacked by a swarm of killer bees?"

"No!" She grabbed the phone back. "That's not the point. I got this message even though I don't have any airtime. And there's no return number."

"Telemarketers have mysterious ways, don't they?"

"Come on, Martin. Don't you see? This message is from the tree."

Was she making fun of him? No, she looked nearly frantic—she believed what she was saying. "The tree sent you a text?"

"Why not? It flashed us that message the other day. Things *are* getting worse—you saw what happened in social studies."

"You forgot your homework. So does half the school on any given day." He looked longingly at his oozing sandwich and wished his sloppy joe weren't so, well, sloppy. Made it hard to eat it around Hannah. He ate a chip instead.

"But not me! I never forget," she said. "That's only the start of it. This is getting scary. I feel like the trees are watching me. A branch from the tree next to our house cracked my window the other night. That dead grass all around Chase on the field, the broken scoreboard, the way the bees attacked you." The hairs rose on the back of Martin's neck—that was just how he felt. Hannah dropped her voice and said, "I had the strangest dream last night. And when I woke up, I started getting messages over a disconnected phone."

Martin remembered what Jenna had told him in the midst of his antihistamine daze. "The other day Jenna said something about plants sending out electronic or magnetic signals."

Hannah nodded. "And those bees. They're social animals—they communicate with chemical signals, different flying patterns. Don't tell me that attack was a coincidence."

"I was standing on their hive. They were kind of provoked." Martin used a chip to scoop up some sandwich filling.

"Maybe. But look at my phone. If the tree could flash a message, if it could send out electrical or radio signals, then it fits. Why *couldn't* the tree send messages over the airwaves now?"

"Now we just need Jenna to help us, after we practically broke into her house."

"It was just her beehive, Martin," Hannah said. "We can win her over, and she's forgotten more about trees than we will ever know. So, if she's not behind the whole curse thing, she can figure out who is."

"A witch can be a good person to have on your side."

Hannah wrinkled her freckled nose. "I told you I don't like that word."

"It's not like it's a bad thing. You know, back in the old days, ignorant villagers used to be afraid of wise women— the women who understood plants and medicines. They called them witches, too. People are afraid of what they don't understand." Martin couldn't wait anymore. He took a huge bite of sandwich, sloppy joe sauce squirting between his fingers. At least it landed on the tray.

"Well, no wonder this is creeping me out," Hannah said, looking creeped out by Martin now, too. "Because heck if I can understand any of this. But don't worry, I will."

19

Junior Junior Executives of Tomorrow

After school Martin felt the full effects of his bad luck when he was forced to attend his first Junior JET meeting. It was even worse than he expected. First, Aunt Michelle insisted he wear a suit. A suit! As if he really were some sort of mini-executive.

"Always dress to impress, Martin," she said, practically shooing him upstairs when she saw what he was wearing—his favorite T-shirt, some perfectly decent cargo shorts (only slightly frayed), and his second-best pair of running shoes that had been promoted to the most presentable since his new pair lost that run-in with a pile of unidentified crap.

He was still grumbling when he came downstairs in his too-small suit. For a moment he had been pleased to have grown out of it; then he saw the twitch in Aunt Michelle's temple.

"I suppose I'm not surprised your mother didn't think to buy you a new suit since Grandmother's funeral this summer," she said with disgust. Martin would have snapped at her, but his nose began to twitch a little at the blunt mention of Abuelita, and he had to concentrate on not crying. He would not let his emotions out, not in front of

Aunt Michelle. She noticed the look on his face and said, "Oh, don't worry, sweetie. We'll get you a new suit this weekend."

As if the suit was what bothered him. As if shopping with his aunt was consolation instead of punishment. Instead he muttered, "What's wrong with what I was wearing? If it's good enough for school, shouldn't it be good enough for after-school activities?"

"Just 'good enough' is never good enough, Martin. Junior Junior Executives of Tomorrow is not just an after-school activity. It's where today's boys and girls meet their selves of tomorrow."

Like everything else Aunt Michelle said, it sounded like it ought to be carved on some dumb plaque and hung on the wall. And when Martin walked into the Greater Brynwood Community Center, it was the first thing he saw written on a plaque above the whiteboard.

WHERE TODAY'S BOYS AND GIRLS MEET THEIR SELVES OF TOMORROW

At least I know where she got that lame saying from, he thought, taking a seat by the window. He left his iPod on and tried to sneak a look around before anyone noticed him. He didn't recognize anybody, but that was no surprise. Then he saw the girl who had been hanging out with Hannah's friend, Whatshername. The girl with the social studies textbook who didn't like to share. The girl who was always staring at him, laughing as if she'd just said something he wouldn't want to hear. Libby.

Oh crap. She spotted him.

And even worse, she was walking his way, flinging her shiny hair around like she was in a shampoo commercial.

She sat down next to him, toying with a lock of hair and smiling dazzlingly with her clear braces. "Aren't you Hannah's friend, Marvin?"

"Martin, actually." He prepped himself for some juvenile mean-girl joke.

"I'm so sorry," she said. And she actually looked disappointed. "Last week in Junior JET we practiced remembering names for our first lesson. When you know someone's name, you're halfway to knowing them. Or something. The secret is using a mnemonic device. You associate a person with an object or phrase, and that helps you remember their name."

"What was mine?"

"Marvin Martian, of course. You know, the way your hair sort of sticks out from your head. But mostly your voice."

He should have known better than to ask. What made it worse was that she was trying to be nice, and this was the best she could do.

"I'm Libby, in case you didn't know," she said, as if she thought he would know. Which he did. She offered her hand, but he must have grabbed too soon because he squeezed her fingers in a weird, limp handshake. "Waverly wasn't sure about you, but if you're friends with Hannah and a Junior JET, maybe you're okay." She paused as if she expected a response, like thanks. When Martin didn't say anything, she continued, "There aren't many Lower Brynwood kids here, actually. Just a couple of us from Brynwood Estates. The rest is an Upper Brynwood crowd, so I'll introduce you. My parents are lawyers, and they think this will give me an edge for my college interviews. What about you?"

"My Aunt Michelle made me come."

"You mean Michelle Medina? She's scheduled to be a guest speaker soon. I didn't know you were related. She's chairman of the board for JET! Did you know she was the one who started the junior version of Junior Executives of Tomorrow?"

Martin gave her a sideways look. "She didn't mention that, exactly. I thought she was in the club back in high school."

Libby squealed with delighted exasperation. "It's not a club. It's an honor society, and yeah, it's been around for, like, a hundred years. She just started the middle school version. That's why we have her quoted up there." She jabbed her blue-manicured thumb towards the plaque hanging over the whiteboard.

Martin thunked his elbows on the desk and laced his fingers over the top of his head. It figured.

Libby twirled a lock of her hair. "So, do you want my notes from last week?"

"That's okay."

She nodded. "This week is when the good stuff starts—the Seven Habits of Highly Successful Executives. One habit per week. We're starting with *Superbia*."

"Suburbia?"

"No, *Superbia*. That's Latin for pride. If you're proud of yourself, you attract the respect you deserve. That sort of thing."

"Sounds awesome. Good thing I've got all my pencils sharpened," Martin said, opening his bag. He contemplated the perfect point of one yellow pencil and remembered how, as a ranger, he'd once used a stiletto to stab his own eardrums, avoiding the trap of an Arlithean mountain siren's deadly song. Not a bad backup plan, except that he didn't have a trove of hit points and Marlician heal-all herb to reverse deafness once class was over. Then again, if he had Marlician heal-all herb, this whole Spirit Tree problem would solve itself. Or not.

A fortyish woman with heavy makeup and long, perfect soap-opera hair stepped in front of the class and cleared her throat so that Martin could hear the phlegm rattling around in the back. She may have only been trying to get the group's attention, but she managed to gross Martin out at the same time.

"Ms. Stemmler," Libby said, leaning in closer. Her hair smelled like tropical fruit. "She's a corporate trainer during the day. I think she's a secret smoker."

Martin wouldn't have been surprised if a loogie came shooting out when Ms. Stemmler opened her mouth to speak. He got the impression that middle-school students—even neatly dressed, well-behaved ones—made her gag, and the feeling, for him, was mutual.

Martin's mind wandered to how Hannah had done in her soccer game. He hoped she'd won. Crap, at this rate, he hoped her leg didn't fall off or an asteroid didn't crash in midfield.

Then Martin started to draw, and before long he didn't notice the droning in his ears. He forgot about Hannah, too. It was only later that he noticed the Wise Woman he drew on his notepad had a freckled nose, a heart-shaped face, and a long ponytail down her back.

Martin ran through a field beneath an open sky.

At least, he thought it was a field. He saw that this had been a forest, but now the trees lay around him, tossed like pick-up sticks. As he climbed along the trail, he dodged massive spokes of twisted roots, upended and ripped from the ground as if the trees had swung on hinges, opening muddy pits where they had stood.

A glistening pink earthworm dripped from a lid of earth. Martin realized the trees must have just fallen, although their bark was so ghostly they looked long dead.

Martin ran. His heart pounded, but not because he was afraid. He climbed the path that followed Mill Creek, bridged now by dozens of fallen trunks crisscrossed at mad angles that reminded Martin of the junction of superhighways.

The Spirit Tree still stood at the highest point of the hill—Martin's destination. The beech's moss-flocked branches nearly obscured the moon, which had risen directly behind it.

Martin ran to the tree, his hand stretched out to touch the trunk as always. He felt only air. As he reached for it, the bark moved away faster than he was running. The tree was falling.

The earth heaved beneath his feet, levering him into mid-air. Martin scrambled backwards off the ledge of soil. He fell hard to the ground, a twelve-foot drop. The wrenching, shrieking sound of splitting wood filled Martin's ears and brain. The ground shook with an impact, and then there was silence—not a bird, not a cricket, not the whoosh of a car on the highway just over the hill.

Martin stood, testing his bruised limbs, and surveyed the littered moonscape around him.

The last tree had fallen. The woods were gone.

Martin woke to the screeching of chairs. His head jerked up, but for a moment he didn't know where he was, surrounded by a bunch of kids dressed up like it was a funeral. Then Libby grabbed his arm and leaned towards him. Oh, yeah, Junior JET.

"Wasn't that great?" she said. "I'll see you tomorrow at school, Martin."

Martin nodded blankly and wiped a trickle of drool out of the corner of his mouth that he hoped she hadn't noticed.

Libby followed the flow of chattering kids out the door, but Martin took his time gathering his things. His head was thick with fog, and he had a feeling Aunt Michelle was going to make him wait.

20

Wide Reach

Hannah did a double take when she walked into the cafeteria. Martin was squeezed in between Waverly and Libby, who seemed to be talking at once while he stared straight ahead. Hannah hadn't spoken to Wave the day before. Her old friend gave her a tentative smile, but Libby flashed a million-dollar grin, white teeth behind clear braces.

"You've been holding out on us, Hannah," Libby said, grasping Martin's ropy forearm and giving it a squeeze. "Martin's pretty cool. We're both Junior JET. Did you know his aunt is in charge of the whole thing?"

Martin shrugged, but she didn't release him, holding on to his arm as if she owned him. "She made me go," he mumbled. "It's some kind of future business leaders thing."

"Junior Junior Executives of Tomorrow. I've been begging Waverly to join, too."

"My dad says I can't add new extra-curriculars until I get my grades up," said Waverly, shifting uncomfortably. "Maybe next quarter."

"What about you, Hannah?" asked Libby. "You want to join us? Martin must have mentioned it."

"No, he didn't. But I can't. I have soccer." Hannah felt wary.

"Oh, yeah," said Martin, looking eager to change the subject. Probably eager to eat his lunch, too. He pulled his arm from Libby and picked up a fork. "How was the game?"

"They won. Hannah scored two goals," Waverly answered, her eyes flicking away when Hannah smiled. "What? I saw it online."

She looked it up! She can't be mad anymore, Hannah thought.

"Awesome. Well, when the season's over, think about joining," Libby said. "Martin and I could use someone like you."

Martin and Libby? Hannah thought. Yesterday Libby had sneered at him like he was gum on her shoe, and today she was hanging on his arm like they had just won a dating-show trip to Puerto Vallarta. If there were two people with less in common, she didn't know them. Then again, maybe she didn't know Martin at all. She had thought he was different from everyone else in Lo-B, but maybe he was just waiting for his chance to prove he was the same.

Hannah didn't listen to what Libby was saying, but Waverly laughed hysterically and Martin set his mouth in a grim line, even while chewing. Hannah breathed a sigh of relief to know that sitting here made him miserable. That was the Martin she knew.

He raked a hand through his hair, making it even wilder. Hannah noticed the tiny, tight curls along his hairline—they looked almost fuzzy, and she had a strange impulse to touch them. Martin caught her looking at him and rolled his eyes at whatever Libby had been saying. Yep, that was her Martin.

She smiled, and then she laughed along with Waverly, without knowing the joke. If the four of them could sit together, that sure would make life easier.

She was already on the trail of a tree killer, and she didn't need any other enemies, especially not one as formidable as

Libby Cho-Johnson. And especially not one she knew and loved as well as Waverly, no matter how different they were.

The school day couldn't end soon enough, but as soon as it did, Hannah found herself longing for soccer practice instead of another afternoon with Martin. Soccer was easy, at least for her. There were rules. She could predict what was about to happen before it did—where the ball was going, which direction the goalie would leap. Easy.

Ever since she met Martin, the rules in her real life didn't make sense. Trees could talk. Libby hung out with nerds. And Hannah didn't have a best friend. For the first time in a long time, she didn't know what to do, but somehow she ended up mixed up with Martin.

As they bounded up the trail through the park after school, Hannah finally worked up the guts to ask what she'd been wondering all day. "So, how did you end up buddies with Libby?"

"Beats me. She sat next to me at that dumb junior middle-manager event, and it was all over. I guess it's like having the Good Housekeeping seal stamped on my forehead."

"What was the meeting like?"

"Boring. Creepy. But so is everything around here."

Hannah was about to defend her hometown, but she decided to let it drop for once.

The leaf cover overhead had thinned slightly, letting sunshine stream through where the path had been shadowed the week before. Poison ivy blazed brilliant red, licking up tree trunks like flames. The woods were noisier, too. Leaves crunched on the path, and the sound of the creek was louder without the brush cover. The drier leaves rustled like wind chimes in the breeze. Hannah remembered her dream and hoped the woods weren't really dying like the Spirit

Tree, not to mention those Bradford pears and every lawn in town. She always thought trees seemed more alive during autumn—storing up food, closing up shop for the winter, throwing a bon voyage party until spring.

Not the Spirit Tree. She could feel it fading, and from a distance it looked oddly indistinct. The air shimmered around it like a heat mirage as they approached. Hannah's heart lifted when she realized the tree had company.

It wasn't hard to spot Jenna through the brush. She glowed in a hideous neon green and orange unitard and a molded helmet—at least she wouldn't have to worry about illegal hunters mistaking her for a deer. Hannah noticed a trail bike on the ground and realized Jenna's Cirque du Soleil get-up was a bike outfit.

"She's here!" Hannah said, quickening her steps. "I knew she couldn't resist helping the tree when we told her what we were doing."

"That's only because she doesn't know what we're really up to," Martin said, trailing behind.

"Well, we don't want her thinking we're the kind of lunatics who talk to trees."

"Except we are."

"Only when they talk to us first," Hannah said. She wouldn't have believed it if it hadn't happened to her, but she couldn't ignore her own senses.

Please don't let Jenna be the bad one, thought Hannah as she headed toward Jenna and the tree. Hannah had always wanted to be a scientist, but she hadn't even understood what they did. Jenna was the first one she'd really met, except her teachers and Dr. Wiggins, if optometrists counted as scientists. Once Libby told her behind Waverly's back that he didn't even count as a real doctor, but Hannah didn't believe her.

"Hey, Dr. Blitzer!" Hannah called out. "So, you're going to help?"

"I guess you captured my interest," Jenna said, grinning back. "I wanted to see this tree myself."

When Hannah and Martin came closer, Jenna inspected him for signs of bee stings. He looked like he was trying very hard not to squirm away from her grip.

"So, what do you think of the Spirit Tree?" Hannah asked.

"It's breathtaking," Jenna said. She let go of Martin's arm and gestured toward the tree's crown. Hannah couldn't help checking to make sure nothing was about to crash down on them. Halfway up, the broad, fluted trunk split into five trunks, each as wide and tall as any of the neighboring trees. Its leaves were mostly green, but gilded where the tree touched the sky.

"It's really old, isn't it?" Martin asked, scratching a welt on his arm that he hadn't seemed to notice before Jenna reminded him of it.

She nodded. "This magnificent old tree is an American beech, *Fagus grandifolia.* It's a tough tree to cut down, so loggers often left them standing even when they mowed down everything else."

"So sad—poor trees," said Hannah. She couldn't help thinking of trees as sentient now.

"The settlers didn't see it that way," said Jenna. "You know, Hannah, the relationship between plants and the human environment is what we landscape ecologists study. My job with the university extension office is promoting sustainable land use, so I can understand why the settlers cleared the forest. They needed sunny farmland for crops and timber for homes and fuel."

"So this used to be farmland, Dr. Blitzer?" Martin asked. "I don't know how anybody got a plow up this hill."

"They probably didn't," Jenna said. She began circling the tree in her funny-looking bike shoes. "This land is too steep. There was a mill on the creek below where the farmers ground their wheat into flour and Thomas Brynwood made his fortune. This hillside may have been cleared for timber for the mill or surrounding homes. It may have been burned for fuel. But the Spirit Tree stood when the mill fell."

"So you do remember the beech being called that?" Hannah said, jumping on her word choice. "Being called the Spirit Tree, I mean."

"No, but I remember coming to these woods with my high-school environmental club and admiring it. It wasn't carved then. We just wanted to see it—bear witness to a tree that had borne witness. There aren't too many old trees around anymore. And if I'm right about this one, it could be more unusual than you think."

I doubt that very much, Hannah thought to herself.

"These are called arborglyphs—tree writing," she said, tracing a carved line with her blunt fingernail.

"It's mutilation," Martin said, stripping off his backpack and tossing it to the ground harder than he needed to.

"Some historians consider arborglyphs a form of artwork," Jenna said. Her blue eyes had been bright, but now the line between them deepened. "American Indians made them, and Basque immigrant sheepherders marked the aspen forests out west as a living record of their presence. I know plant ecologists who study culturally modified trees to gain insight into North American culture and human relationships with the environment. Some carvings are quite beautiful."

"Not these," said Martin.

"I agree. This is graffiti," Jenna said, placing a palm on the tree. "Poor hapless beeches attract vandals because of the smooth bark. Then cuts in the surface make them vulnerable to beech scale insects and then beech bark disease, a fungal infection that can kill the tree."

"Is there a cure?" Hanna said.

"It's hard to control," Jenna said. "The chemicals are risky, only worthwhile for high-value trees. But this tree might be worth it. Have you ever heard of a Champion Tree?"

Hannah and Martin shook their heads.

"State and national arbor societies keep a registry of the biggest trees of each species. This one's got to be over a hundred feet tall. That's knocking on the record books, so this tree might be worth saving."

"Then you will cure it?" Hannah asked again, impatient for her to get to the point.

"Slow down. I don't know for sure that it's a record holder, and I don't know for sure that it's suffering from beech bark disease. It could just be old—at least two hundred fifty years, from the looks of it. Nothing lives forever—not even a tree." She glanced around. "This whole woodland looks stressed, to tell the truth. There's a lot less undergrowth than I'd expect, so anything could be wrong—invasive insects, factory runoff. This isn't exactly a thriving ecosystem. I'll take some samples, talk to my colleagues, and we'll find out." She pulled out a kit from her backpack and began to collect—twigs neatly lined with ridged leaves, a sample of silvery bark from a few carvings. To Hannah, it looked like she was working in slow motion.

"When will you know?" she asked, unable to hold it in. "We don't have that much time."

Jenna patted her hand. "Maybe not, but the tree can wait. Trees don't live forever, but they don't die overnight, either. Trees don't care if you hurry."

Hannah thought of the text message the Spirit Tree had sent saying just the opposite, and shook her head.

Martin pulled her off to one side and whispered to her, "So, we agree there's no way Jenna cursed the tree?"

She nodded. "She's a scientist. She wouldn't even believe in curses," she said, remembering that she had felt the same way a few weeks earlier. "But she can help heal the tree if it can be fixed with some kind of antifungal spray or something." If the beech was suffering from an ordinary disease, they could heal it. But what if the problem really was magic? Hannah wasn't sure a spray would work.

Jenna had stepped closer to the tree and was examining the bark at close range.

"Do you recognize any of the messages written in the carvings?" Hannah asked, waving her hand near the carving of the six Es in the hope that Jenna would notice it.

"Hmm? No. If I had known this graffiti was happening back when I was in high school, I would have brought the whole environmental club out here with pickets and chained myself to the trunk."

"What was the name of your club?" said Hannah, watching for signs of guilt.

Jenna laughed a little. "Let's see, Environmental Economy, Ecological Enterprise, Energy Efficiency... something like that. I made sure it had six Es because I thought that would be snappy. It was just a mouthful."

"Six Es? You mean like those Es there?" Hannah pointed to the carving overtly now.

"Environment, Ecology, and Energy Efficiency for an Enlightened Earth—that's it!" Jenna said, snapping her fingers.

"So, is that what those Es are for?" Hannah tried to focus Jenna's attention.

Jenna finally noticed the letters in the bark. "I doubt it. Nobody from my club would have carved it. Besides, they're not Es." Jenna pointed to the jagged line in the middle of each. "They're sigmas."

Hannah and Martin both looked closer. They had just thought they were chiseled crudely, but now the intent was clear. They weren't letters—they were symbols.

"What's a sigma?" she said.

"It's a Greek letter," Martin answered. "Like fraternities use."

"Scientists use them, too," Jenna said. "Sigma represents the rate of change. Although I don't think a scientist would carve it on the tree—looks more like a fraternity prank to me."

Hannah realized they'd shown up at Jenna's door because of a clue that they'd figured completely wrong. But it didn't matter if they'd come to Jenna for the wrong reasons. She was turning out to be just the help they needed.

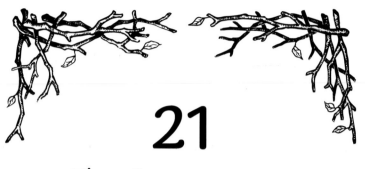

21

The Conversation

When Jenna was gone, Martin turned to Hannah. He could hardly get the words out fast enough. "We should have known the curse was some stupid frat ritual. Brainless high-school jocks grow up into brainless college frat boys. First they carve the tree, then they dress up in hooded robes and pour sacrificial blood on the roots."

"Martin, please," Hannah said. "It's not like Lower Brynwood has packs of frat brothers roaming the streets. Where would they go to college, anyway? A.J. took a semester of classes at the community college, and if there had been fraternities, he wouldn't have dropped out so fast."

Martin sniffed, deliberately missing the point. "Not like the love of learning and knowledge could have kept him."

"A.J. is smart, Martin, even if he doesn't know it. If he had felt more connected, he might have stayed."

Martin felt a twinge—A.J. actually seemed all right. But he couldn't help railing against the frat boys of the world, although he hadn't actually met any of them. "If you're a strong enough person, you don't need to join clubs to buy yourself friends."

"You mean clubs like Junior JET?" Hannah said, raising an eyebrow. "How seriously can you take a club that sounds like one of Thomas the Tank Engine's buddies?"

"I'm not taking it seriously," Martin said, feeling his ears turning red. He hoped she wouldn't notice. "And they're not my friends."

"Really? That's not how Libby acted." Hannah crossed her arms.

"You didn't care what Libby did yesterday. Why should you care now?" Martin's whole face burned. She couldn't be jealous, could she?

"Enough. We know we've been barking up the wrong tree." Hannah paused, glaring at Martin as if to warn him not to laugh at her accidental pun. He wouldn't dare. "So it looks like Jenna's off the hook. But we still don't know what Sigma Sigma Sigma Sigma, uh…" She looked at her fingers, counting silently, "…Sigma Sigma is. And this time I know who to ask."

"You're the town expert. Who?"

"Ever heard of Professor Google? Does that iPod of yours show any Wi-Fi in range?"

Martin's hand flew to the pocket that held the gadget. "No," he said. "At least, there's no way I'm going to get a signal out here in the woods."

An electronic hum broke the silence, coming right from Martin's pocket. Impossible, but he felt it leap to life under his hand.

"Aren't you going to answer that? I think you have a call," Hannah asked.

"I told you, it's not a phone. It's just an old iPod."

The tone buzzed again, more insistent this time.

"Then you have an instant message," Hannah said. "If you don't want to answer, at least shut it off."

She wasn't going to give up. He pulled it out gently.

"Your iPod!" Hannah said, looking distressed. "It's broken—the curse again."

He bit his lip, but shook his head no. "It dropped out of my pocket and I rode the bike over it. I didn't want you to know. But it doesn't matter. It was already broken."

"Ah," she said, nodding. "So that's why you haven't been wearing it lately."

"You don't understand," he said, fitting the case back together with a sense of desperation. "It never worked. My mom gave it to me when she left for Afghanistan, but I broke it." He had accidentally dropped it in a toilet, but he wouldn't tell Hannah that.

"But you always wear it."

He shrugged. "I didn't want anyone to talk to me." *I didn't want anyone to notice that no one wanted to talk to me,* he thought. He didn't like the way Hannah was looking at him now—as if she was sorry for him. That's just what he didn't want when he moved to this stupid town. He'd been the new kid often enough in his life.

The iPod buzzed again, the noise rattling through the broken case. The screen glowed with golden light.

Hannah looked triumphant. "If your iPod is broken, what is it doing?"

"I don't know."

"It's the tree again!" she said.

A message filled the screen. Martin held it so Hannah could read, too.

I'M HOLDING ON. DON'T LET ME DOWN.

The Spirit Tree, he thought. *It really is the tree.* He put his hand back to the bark and looked at the spokes of branches above.

"O mighty tree…" Martin said. He expected Hannah to mock him, but her eyes were wide. She laid her cheek against the rough bark.

"O mighty tree," she said, softly, "we won't let you down. Who did this? How do we stop it?"

Martin looked at the phone expectantly, then shook it. It hummed to life with a yellow blaze.

HUMANS ALL LOOK THE SAME.

Martin frowned. Yeah, he and Chase were dead ringers all right.

BUT YOU EACH FEEL DIFFERENT. I SENSE YOU AND THE BOY WHEREVER YOU ARE.

"I knew it," Martin said. "The tree has been spying on us." He should have been amazed to be communicating with an inanimate object, but instead he felt vindicated. He had known the tree was watching. Waiting. Like in his bedroom that first night, and whenever he set foot in the forest. The Spirit Tree knew he was coming.

"Can you sense who did this to you?" Hannah asked, her voice as gentle as if she were talking to a child. She kept one hand on the tree but her eyes on the bright screen.

Martin didn't have the patience for this tree-whispering act. "Who? When?" he asked. "Where is he now?"

IT HURTS TO SENSE THE BAD ONE.

"Don't try," said Hannah, patting the bark. "We're getting close. This will be over soon."

The golden glow faded. The cracks in the iPod spidered outward, the plastic shell shattered. Only Martin's grip held it together now. The device was destroyed, and it looked as if it would never work again.

"So, that's that," Martin said, then smiled.

"What are you smiling about?" Hannah asked, sounding curious, not accusing.

"The tree really spoke. It really texted us." Anything was possible—the boundaries of what was real and what was fantasy were strangely porous. Martin was a ranger for real.

22

The Sentence

Being a seventh-grade ranger had drawbacks. The whole town teetered on the whim of some evil curseworker, but Martin and Hannah had to sit in school all day like good little schoolchildren.

Martin couldn't even talk to Hannah alone. That Junior JET thing managed to ruin not just the four hours a week that he spent there, but every other free moment during the school day. Libby flagged him down in the hallway. She perched on the edge of his desk in social studies. She plopped down next to him in the lunchroom—always with Waverly in tow.

He tried to ditch Libby, but answering in monosyllables didn't work. He tried snarky comebacks, but she thought he was hilarious. At least Hannah laughed at his jokes, too, so it wasn't a total waste. She wasn't much like Gord or Zach, but she was cool.

But on Wednesday Hannah had soccer practice, and Martin was sure she wouldn't skip it for anything, not even the tree. He ran out to the Spirit Tree by himself, probably his best mile pace ever, but it wasn't the same. When he got to the top of the hill, he touched the bark with his hand and spoke aloud. "O mighty tree."

Nothing. Martin didn't have his iPod to tune into messages, and more importantly, he didn't have Hannah. When she was beside him, the air crackled with electricity—the tree hummed on a frequency so strong he could almost hear it. But when she wasn't there, it felt like just another ordinary tree—an old, battle-scarred tree ready to fall down in the slightest breeze.

On Thursday Hannah told him to meet at her locker after school instead of the west exit. He couldn't wait to get back to work, and he couldn't help being pleased that now she didn't mind being seen with him in front of everyone. At least Martin had that.

When they got to Aunt Michelle's house, a big-headed man leaned against a massive SUV parked in the stamped-concrete driveway. He balanced a clipboard against the beginning of a paunch, flexing meaty biceps as he wrote. Martin didn't like the look of him, and not just because he stood in the way of their entry.

"Oh great," Hannah said, the corners of her mouth tightening.

"You know that guy?" It figured.

"It's A.J.'s boss, Jake Laughlin. I asked him to take a look at the tree, remember? Kind of a jerk, but if he knows his trees, maybe he can help."

"I'd be surprised if he knew his ABCs."

"Well, he says he's a tree surgeon. Anyway, the more we know about how to heal the tree, the better. Plus, he's one of the football coaches and he used to play, so he probably knows the history of the Spirit Tree ceremony. And now's as good a time as any to ask him," she said, then called out, in a sunny voice that seemed to convey delighted surprise, "Mr. Laughlin! What are you doing here?"

He crunched a mint between his teeth and said, "Hi there, uh, little Vaughan. Just a courtesy call on my best customer. What brings you here?"

"I do," Martin said, stepping between them. "I live here."

Jake looked him over suspiciously, and Martin felt color rising to the roots of his curly hair. "You couldn't be Michelle's son." As if he suspected Martin of running a junior burglary ring.

"I'm just her second cousin. But I'm living here for a while."

"Lucky kid. She's a very special woman," Jake said, then popped another mint in his mouth without offering the tin. Martin couldn't think of any response, since agreement was out of the question.

"Yeah," Hannah said, nearly elbowing Martin out of the way to talk. Fine with Martin. "But we're the lucky ones, finding you here. Martin's my partner on the Spirit Tree project. We were researching plant diseases, and we have some more questions for you about what might be stressing the Spirit Tree."

"That's a funny way of putting it," Jake said, snorting. "Like a plant could feel stressed out. You've heard the expression 'vegged out'? Where do you think it comes from?"

"It's not funny," said Hannah, lifting her pointed chin. "I just meant stressed, like it needed more water or had an insect infestation. And plants *do* react to danger. We've even heard that trees and plants in distress send out signals."

"Be glad they don't," he said, eyeballing Martin as if he expected a fellow guy to laugh along with him. Martin didn't smile, but Jake kept riffing. "I already know what lawns would say. Feed me. Water me. Mow me. Edge me. But I don't take orders from plants—I show them who's boss."

"I'm serious," said Hannah, furrowing her brow deeper. "Phytochemical markers, electromagnetic vibrations, that sort of thing. Some scientists have picked up ultrasonic vibrations with lie detectors."

Jake leaned in, and Martin got a whiff of something sour under the menthol. "And do the plants lie?" Jake said.

"Of course not. What we mean is, some people think they communicate, like if they are injured or endangered."

"I've never heard that, and I started cutting lawns when I was your age. Never thought I'd do it for a living, but here I am, a tree surgeon for the past five years. Never had a patient complain once." Jake straightened up to his full height, and for a second he looked almost professional to Martin instead of like just another overgrown frat boy. Then Jake cracked himself up. "Maybe I just can't hear them screaming over the sound of my chainsaw."

"You don't have to make fun of us," Hannah said, crossing her arms. "If you're a tree surgeon, don't you even care about trees?"

"You wouldn't like plants so much if you spent your days cleaning up after them like I do," Jake said, frowning so that his thick brows nearly touched. "You kids are so susceptible to all that stuff those tree huggers made up, like global warming." Hannah tried to catch Martin's eye, but Martin just shook his head. He didn't expect any better from Jake, who had probably bullied kids just like Martin back in the day. "Figures. Leave it to tree huggers to think the world is a greenhouse."

Martin's jaw dropped. "Didn't you study any of this in school?" he asked. "A.J. said he wanted to take classes to get certified as an arborist."

"Forget classes," Jake spat. "Who needs certification? Tree surgery ain't brain surgery. Mostly amputations and euthanasia, the way I do it."

Martin exchanged a worried look with Hannah. They should never have involved this guy. "We can see you're really busy, Jake," Hannah said, smiling weakly. "Maybe it's better if you don't look at the Spirit Tree, after all."

"Already did," said Jake. "Good thing you called me when you did."

"Why? Do you think you can save the tree?" Hannah said, a little hope in her voice. Martin felt nothing but dread.

Jake waved her off. "It's not worth it. I already recommended to the township that the tree be cut down, and the sooner the better."

23

Professor Google

Martin crumpled up Jake's invoice as soon as he slammed the door behind him.

"I can't believe it," he said, clenching his fists, trying to stay in control as he paced the hall. "That tree butcher has no idea what he's doing. Guys like that carved the tree up, then they chop it down when it's too weak to take anymore. It's a death sentence."

"Not if we can stop it," Hannah said, so calmly that Martin felt ashamed of himself. He tried to think, but he felt as if his whole body was about to explode.

"What can we do? Jake already put in the work request. He said he was going to get it fast-tracked, whatever that means. Next time we see the Spirit Tree, it'll be mulching Aunt Michelle's shrubs." Martin shuddered, thinking of Jake's wood chipper. It was like imagining a dismembered body buried in the yard.

"Calm down. We'll think of something. We still haven't figured out what the inscriptions mean. If we can solve the puzzle before the work order comes in, we can save the tree."

Martin took a breath, the way his mom had taught him. Take a breath, count to ten. He couldn't let Jake throw him off. "All right. Let's get to work."

Hannah followed him into Aunt Michelle's home office, which had an oversized window overlooking the yard. Jake still lurked outside. He put the SUV into gear when he saw Martin glowering at him, backing over the grass on the way out. Martin would have snickered if he weren't so angry. Served Jake right—Aunt Michelle would freak when she saw tire tracks on the lawn. Some courtesy call.

Martin typed in his password. A *Dragon Era* discussion board popped up before he could open Google. Crap, he was such a nerd. Not that Hannah would be surprised.

"I saw that," she said, teasing. "So, you play video games. No surprise—so does every guy."

"I guess," Martin said. "I don't even get to play *Dragon Era* since I moved here—the graphics card on this old computer couldn't handle it even if Aunt Michelle let me. I just lurk on the boards so it's almost like I'm playing."

She looked at him as if he was the saddest person on earth. Time to change the subject. He said, "You want to drive, or should I?"

"You can. It's your machine."

He snorted. "My aunt's. The desktop is her backup—it would be powered by a hamster wheel if Aunt Michelle let hamsters in the house. My system wouldn't be anything like this—none of this business crap. Just a gaming package, plus a nice webcam." He'd be able to video chat his mom every day. Martin stopped when Hannah's eyes glazed over. He pecked out the letters, stumbling under her scrutiny, but he only used the backspace key three times.

Sigma sigma sigma sigma sigma sigma.

"No exact matches," he said.

"What about that one?" Hannah pointed to a link for Tri Sigma. "That's pretty close."

The homepage for a sorority alumnae chapter popped up. A group of middle-aged women with round faces and lacquered flip hairdos stood on a staircase straight out of *Gone With The Wind*. Martin whistled. "Scary. They are definitely guilty."

"No way. They look like my mom on her way to church."

"Don't rule them out so quick. You thought Jenna was guilty once, remember?" Martin said, only half-kidding. "Why not a bunch of ex-sorority sisters? Come to think of it, what's your mom's alibi? Mine's in Afghanistan, but yours has had plenty of opportunities to curse the tree."

"Ha ha. My mom is not the revenge type. This might be a joke to you, but that carving is the best lead we have." She glared at him.

"It's not a joke to me," Martin said quietly. Hannah looked into his eyes for a moment and her expression softened. Funny, he always thought her eyes were blue, but up close they were brownish gray, like storm clouds. Nicer than blue.

Her gaze flicked away. "Let's try something else," Hannah said. "If Sigma Sigma Sigma goes by Tri Sig, maybe we should search the inscription another way. Sigma to the sixth power? Sigma times six?"

Martin didn't answer. He just typed.

SIX SIGMA.

As soon as he hit enter, the page filled.

ABOUT 987,000 RESULTS (0.14 SECONDS)

"Bingo. We have a match," he said. He clicked the hypertext for Wikipedia and read aloud in his best news anchor voice: "*Six Sigma is a management strategy implemented by businesses and managers since its initial development in 1981.*" Whatever that meant. He had hoped for some fraternity guys—anything other than business talk.

"That's weird," Hannah said. "Keep going."

"Six Sigma is a process improvement approach that improves quality in manufacturing and business by reducing errors, defects, and variability."

"What does that mean?"

"Don't know. But if it sounds business-y, maybe Aunt Michelle would," he said, swallowing. He looked around the room at Aunt Michelle's Lucite training awards and engraved brass plaques, and had a small, disturbing thought. Six Sigma sounded a lot like something Michelle would talk about. "I'll ask her later." Much later, if he had his way.

Through the door came the sound of a faint jingling—one of the most dreaded sounds on Earth, as far as Martin was concerned. He shut the browser window.

"Hey!" Hannah said. "We're not done yet."

"Yes, we are."

The door creaked open and Aunt Michelle stood there, smirking at them.

"I didn't know you had a little friend over," she said.

"Hannah was just leaving." Martin expected Hannah to scowl at him, but she had switched to cheery talking-to-grownups mode, her bag already slung diagonally across her body.

"Gotta go," she said. "I'll call you later to talk about our project."

Aunt Michelle's smile vanished as soon as Hannah left.

"Martin, I'm glad you have a girlfriend, but only chaperoned visits from now on. If you want to invite her over for a date, the three of us can have a movie night together. I have *You've Got Mail* on DVD—love that Meg Ryan."

He nearly gagged. If that was what it would be like to date Hannah, Martin felt extremely glad it would never happen. Well, mostly glad.

"Sorry I didn't ask first," he said. "Next time we'll go to Hannah's house—it's in the old part of town."

"That's what I was afraid of." Aunt Michelle heaved a sigh. "That kind of girl is fun to hang out with, but you can do better. She'll drag you down. Her brother mows my lawn, for crying out loud. I'm trying to help you overcome your background, but it won't work unless you really want it, Martin."

The heat rose in Martin's face so quickly he felt like his hair was standing up. His mom was risking her life for her country. Even his dad had earned his degree on the G.I. Bill while working two jobs to support him, not to mention his grubby little half-brother. Martin wanted to live up to that, not overcome it.

"Then it won't work," he said. He didn't want anything to do with her or her dumb ideas.

The vein throbbed in Aunt Michelle's temple. "We'll see about that. Better get dressed. Tonight is Junior Junior Executives of Tomorrow, and you're already late."

Anything was better than staying here with Aunt Michelle. He'd go if he had to, but no way would he wear a suit. He would never be one of them.

24

Slow Walk

Hannah couldn't let it go. Jake had laughed at her when she talked about the tree. He might be an idiot and a bully, but being mocked by an idiot was more humiliating because she ought to be able to defend herself. But she couldn't tell the truth, because everyone knew trees didn't talk. She wasn't Alice in Wonderland. She didn't believe in impossible things. But still, the tree had texted her. Anything she could observe was real, and she'd find a logical explanation. Or a semi-logical one. Or at least an explanation.

She fired up the ancient computer in the kitchen as her mom chopped vegetables and seasoned ground meat for dinner. The machine cranked, and Hannah groaned along with it. She cracked open a plant ecology textbook from the library. Cross-referencing the book and the web, she set to work on a scientific timeline, writing as neatly as possible.

1747—Jean Antoine Nollet, physics tutor to the French dauphin, studied electromagnetism in plants. When he electrified seeds (LIKE WITH LIGHTNING???) they grew faster, and when he electrified plants, the water moved more quickly through their vascular systems.

1859—London Gardener's Chronicle *reported that light flashed from one scarlet verbena to another before a thunderstorm (JUST LIKE THE SPIRIT TREE!!!). They said the earth has a negative electrical charge and atmosphere positive. Usually electrons stream up from soil and plants, but during storms the polarity reverses and it goes the other way.*

1900s—*Sir Jagdish Chandra Bose, Indian scientist, found that every plant responded to stimulation. When he shocked plants with electricity, they had spasms, just like animal muscles. When he played pleasant music his plants grew faster, and when he treated them harshly they grew slower. (IS THAT HOW THE CURSE HURTS THE TREE?)*

1920s—*Georges Lakhovsky, Russian scientist, thought living cells were electromagnetic radiators that emitted and absorbed high-frequency waves. He said they were circuits with stored electric charges. (LIKE A CELL PHONE?)*

1960s—*Cleve Backster, American scientist, attached a polygraph (lie detector) to a philodendron to measure water resistance. The tracing looked just like a person's!!! (IF PLANTS REACT TO SPEECH, THEY CAN UNDERSTAND IT!)*

Before she could get to the 1970s, her mom told her to set the table for dinner.

Usually Taco Night was Hannah's favorite meal at the Vaughan house, but tonight she just wanted to get back to research. Her cat was impatient, too, tugging at her sneaker laces. Distracted, she misjudged her first bite, shattering the hard corn shell and dumping shredded lettuce all over her lap and the floor. Tacos weren't the best food to eat when her mind was elsewhere. Too bad Vincent Vaughan Gogh didn't like Mexican food.

"You're quiet tonight," said Hannah's father. "You're not worried about Nick's ball game against Radnor Saturday, are you?"

Nick grunted but didn't look up from his playbook as he popped a taco into his mouth with two quick chomps.

The Vaughans gave him an exception to the no-reading-at-dinner rule, and luckily Nick had better taco technique than Hannah did. Or maybe he just had a bigger mouth.

"Andy!" Hannah's mother said, slamming down the fork she was using to eat her taco salad. "Don't you think she's thinking about her own team instead?"

Hannah's father gave her a sheepish look as he spun the lazy Susan to grab the shredded cheese. "Sorry, Hannah Banana," he said. "You do have a demanding schedule for a seventh grader."

"None of you get it," Hannah said, not caring if she sounded bratty. There was more to life than just sports, although if she really thought about it, she *was* worried about both games—probably Nick's more than hers. Her team was doing okay, but the Black Squirrel football team hadn't won yet.

"Something in school, then?" asked Hannah's mother, tilting her head.

"It's got to be that tree thing," said A.J. "Jake told me he'd been out to look at it."

"It's awful," Hannah said, deciding to reconfigure her broken taco into a salad. She picked up her knife and smashed the corn shards into bits with the handle, pounding a little louder than she needed to. "Jake says the tree is too far gone to save. I don't believe him."

"Well, like it or not, I have to trust him," said Nick. "I'm not going to win a scholarship without him. Plus, you couldn't stand that Martin kid last week."

"I didn't know him then," Hannah said. "And he was right. You and your buddies carved up that tree up like it was Thanksgiving dinner, and now Jake's going to chop it down. He's going to kill it!"

Hannah's mother frowned. "Are you sure he can? It's on public land."

"That's just it," Hannah said, talking louder and faster with every word. "He already filed his bid with the Lower Brynwood Parks Department. Says he's going to have the application fast-tracked, or something. Martin and I only have a couple weeks left to save the tree, and we still have no idea what we're doing."

Hannah's father smiled at his daughter, and she felt like screaming. Hadn't he heard her? Then he said, "Fast-tracked, huh? That application sounds like something that deserves the attention of the Lower Brynwood Assistant Budgetary Manager. Namely, your dear old dad."

"You aren't actually going to help him?" Hannah nearly shouted, but her father waved his hand.

"Of course I'll help him," he said, raising an eyebrow and smiling crookedly. "An application that important needs to be circulated for comment among every assistant manager in every department. Sequentially, of course. Got to check all his credentials and certifications with the state. I'll be sure to distribute it myself. I always like to put it in the in-box of someone who's out of the office for a few days— that way they review it with a nice, fresh attitude. Except when it gets buried under other paperwork. Anyway, if I give Jake's application my personal, fast-track attention, it should make its way toward approval in six to ten weeks. Unless, of course, you come up with a reason that we should deny it before then."

"Dad! You're the best." Hannah stood up and hugged him.

"I always say a bureaucrat can be your best friend or your worst enemy. Like a dad, I guess," he said, hugging her back.

A.J. stared at them. "You all forget that Jake is my boss? He'll blow a gasket if he has to wait that long." He leaned back and grinned. "Awesome."

"Awesome for the rest of you. I'll suffer," said Nick. "When he gets mad, he gives double drills."

"That's not suffering, it's training," said Hannah's father. "Tough drills make tough competitors."

"Now you sound like Coach Laughlin too. All those stupid sayings." Nick scowled.

Hannah wrinkled her brow. "What did you say?"

"Coach always spouts off this inspirational BS about how if you ask the universe for what you want, it answers back. The Answer, he called it." Looking disgusted, Nick shut his notebook and pushed it away. "If the universe was my fairy godmother, a dozen recruiters would be beating down our door."

A.J. nodded. "And I'd be writing my Heisman speech. Or at least I'd be in college."

Their mother gave him a stern look. "It doesn't take a miracle for that, A.J. If you want to go back to community college, all you have to do is register."

"Uh-uh," A.J. said. "Little brother, it's your turn to ask the universe for what you want. I already got my answer: No. I tried to take classes—it didn't work with all the overtime Jake lays on me. I've been busting my hump hauling all the trees that have been keeling over lately. I'm beginning to understand why he hates them so much—I will, too, if I end up working for him much longer. The universe has been throwing a giant bowling ball all over town, and I'm right in its path."

"There's always next semester," Hannah's father said, but he looked puzzled. "Something weird *has* been going on in Lower Brynwood. All those fallen trees, snapped power wires—we had a water main break over on Brynwood-Newtown Pike and another on Route 74. One of the houses under construction in the new public housing development just plain collapsed overnight. Splat. The foreman showed up, and the jobsite looked like a pile of Lincoln Logs. Today we had a street-cleaning vehicle fall into a sinkhole. The ground opened up right underneath the driver. It nearly swallowed him up—he was lucky he wasn't hurt."

Lucky? Hannah thought. It was the opposite of luck—Lower Brynwood was literally crumbling in front of their eyes and under their feet, and the only ones who understood were her, Martin, the tree, and the rotten creep who had cursed the town in the first place. The bad one, whoever that was. Hannah didn't dare look up for fear that someone would notice the tears gathering in her eyes. She had refused to cry in front of her brothers since she was three years old.

She stared at Nick's playbook until she had reabsorbed her tears, and the shape of the leaf embossed on the cover came into focus. Hannah had seen it a thousand times, but this was the first time she recognized the shape.

"Why is that leaf on Nick's playbook?" she asked.

"Good question," A.J. answered, pointing to the matching logo on his shirt. "It's the symbol of Laughlin Landscaping and Tree Care. Good old Jake must be using company property for the benefit of the Lo-B football team—probably took a tax write-off for the donation, too."

Hannah stared at the logo. The leaf was from a beech—just like the Spirit Tree. Jake's logo was the Spirit Tree leaf? Why?

"A.J., Jake used to play football for Lower Brynwood, right?" she asked.

"Are you kidding? He never lets us forget it. He was captain of the team back during the last state championship—heck, during the last winning season we ever had."

"When was that?"

"Ancient history. The golden era of Lower Brynwood sports, 1988 to '89. Four district championship teams in one year, and not one since."

1989? *Forever young, 9/15/1989.* Of course. She should have known. Heck, she was pretty sure Jake's name was written right there on the bark. He must have cursed the tree to guarantee his precious winning season, and just forget everybody who followed him. He designed his whole business around it, and now he was conspiring to take the tree down, once and for all. She and Martin had a new number-one suspect.

All of a sudden Hannah felt famished. Taco Night ruled. She smiled to herself as she filled her fork with taco salad. Martin wouldn't be surprised to hear that the perpetrator— the witch, the bad one, the dark mage, curseworker, whatever—was someone like Jake. And she didn't even care that he was right, as long as they were one step closer to healing the tree. They'd have this mystery wrapped up by Columbus Day.

Slam. A gust of wind banged the loose cellar door. A whirlwind of leaves swirled against the kitchen window, eerie in the purple glow of African-violet plant light.

But the plants under the purple grow lights were dead.

Chair legs screeched on linoleum as Hannah's mother leaped toward the plants. When she touched one dried leaf, it crumbled to dust. Her face crumpled, too, and Hannah thought she would cry.

"Your prize-winning African violets, Mom," Hannah said. Her mom had won a blue ribbon in the garden show three years running.

"How is this possible? They were fine yesterday," Hannah's mother said, her voice catching. Then she switched off the plant light and turned her back, shoulders rounded, walking to the sink to wash her hands. No one spoke.

She dried her hands and returned to the table, her face still and white as marble in the lower light. "Excuse me, kids, for jumping up from the table like that. I'm some example for table manners." She sniffed and toyed with her paper napkin. "It doesn't take much to win a garden-club prize around here," she said. "They were just plants, Hannah.

Next time I'll stick to plastic. Nothing grows here—why would I think I'm so special?"

Later, as Hannah rinsed off the dishes, she noticed how dark the kitchen seemed without the plant light. Lifeless. The windowsill was empty except for the dark rings where the potted violets had sat. Hannah's mother had carried the plant corpses out to the composter with the kitchen scraps. She joked that plants might not grow well in Lower Brynwood, but they sure rotted fast. Everyone laughed, but Hannah couldn't have been the only one who didn't think it was funny. Lower Deadwood, just like Martin called it. Everything died here.

Hannah's mother walked back into the kitchen and wordlessly grabbed a towel to dry the pots dripping in the rack.

"You can let those air-dry overnight, Mom," Hannah said. "I promise to put them away before school."

"Why wait?" Hannah's mother stacked the dry pots and slammed them into the cabinet too hard, setting off a cascade of pot lids against the door as she kicked it shut. She hugged her arms to her chest and leaned against the counter.

"I'm sorry about your violets, Mom."

"They're only plants." Hannah's mom shook her head. "And the garden club eliminated the houseplant category this year, anyway. Michelle Medina said she thought it seemed unhealthy, all that dirt inside." She sniffled. "Poor violets. No surprise they're dead. I can't keep my patients at the nursing home alive, either. Mr. Richardson passed today. I don't think Mrs. Quillen will last another week, either." Her voice caught at the end.

"Maybe it was just their time," Hannah said, knowing how weak it sounded. Something a funeral director would say. "They had good lives. They were really old."

"Two weeks ago they didn't act like it. Mr. Richardson was such a kidder, always giving me a hard time, and Mrs. Quillen dressed like she expected the Queen of England for tea in the residents' lounge. But something changed. Like, overnight. Mr. Richardson didn't recognize me. And Mrs. Quillen came to breakfast one morning, her hair a rat's nest, but worse—her eyes were blank. Now she can't even sit up."

Hannah felt cold in the drafty kitchen. She leaned against the counter next to her mother, resting her head against her mom's shoulder even though they were the same height.

"They're not the only ones," her mom said, sliding an arm around Hannah. "Residents who used to be active just sit there in front of the TV. Catatonic. Mrs. Lee and Mrs. Wallace won't get out of bed. Sometimes they don't know me—it's like an Alzheimer epidemic." Hannah's skin still prickled. "Like all the life that they had just faded away—like it was stolen overnight."

Hannah tried not to think of the curse. Those people were old. Old people got sick. They forgot things. They died.

She looked at the empty shelf where the violets had stood, and at her mother's face, which was so close that she saw wrinkles she had never noticed before. Her mother looked worried and tired. *Old.* Hannah wanted this to be a coincidence—this couldn't be the curse. The curse meant bad luck, dead plants, torn ligaments—it didn't drain the life out of people. Did it?

Her phone blared suddenly. She leaped away from her mother. Thinking of the Spirit Tree, Hannah dug the phone out of her front pocket, afraid of the message it might have sent, relieved that at least the tree was alive to contact her.

The text was from Waverly. Hannah was puzzled. She didn't have any airtime left; at least, none that a human could access.

"That didn't take long," said Hannah's mother, rearranging her worn features into a tiny smile. "Waverly must have some kind of tractor beam on your phone."

"What?" Hannah asked.

"I asked your father to add minutes to your account early. He wasn't due to top up the airtime for two more weeks, but I thought you'd need the phone for your Spirit Tree project."

Hannah gave her mother a quick squeeze, feeling almost normal again. "Thank you!"

"It's only twenty dollars worth—tell Waverly to take it easy or that won't last through the weekend." The phone pinged again. "Waverly again?"

"Who else?" Hannah said. "I'd better reply or she'll send ten more."

"Better yet, pick up the regular phone and save your minutes. I'll finish up here."

Back up in her third-floor room, Hannah read the messages—three of them lined up.

SOMETHING TO TELL U—CALL ME

ITS A SURPRISE—AJ WILL LIKE IT 2—CALL ME

MAB YOU WONT LIKE IT—CALL ME

At first the string of texts annoyed Hannah. As far as Waverly knew, she wouldn't even get them. Hannah guessed sending messages was Waverly's way of thinking something out.

Hannah texted back. WHAT ARE U TALKING ABOUT?

Her cell phone rang immediately.

"Hannah?" Waverly's voice sounded odd.

"That's me."

"I thought your phone was disconnected."

"Then why were you sending messages?"

"Habit, I guess." She paused.

"So?" Hannah asked, exasperated. "You just sent me three messages and called. Is there something you want to tell me?"

"Noooo," she said. "Well, yes, but Libby said to keep it a surprise. We picked a new community history project."

"Really? Isn't it kind of late for that?"

"Maybe, but Libby's parents helped us. Brynwood Park Mall just got condemned. Can you believe it? Some kind of structural damage from a sinkhole, or something—so we figured, what's the point? We're going to unveil our new project at the game tomorrow. You'll like it—it's better than the history of the mall."

"Hopefully you'll get luckier than Martin and me. Did you hear that Jake Laughlin wants to chop the Spirit Tree down?"

Waverly didn't answer right away. "I heard something."

"Ugh. I'd better get back to work."

Once Hannah had knocked off her math homework, she paged through the Spirit Tree notebook. She was amazed how often Jake's name came up, now that she was looking for him.

Jake the Snake

I love Jake

JL + MS

Jake's wasn't the only name—Hannah was surprised how willing vandals were to leave their signatures. Lucky for them that nobody had been trying to track them down until now.

Mark Caputo is a fox

Diane + Mike

Margie Riley is EZ

Saligia rules

The stupidity hurt Hannah's head. She picked up Dr. Wiggins's yearbook from the stack of books on her desk. It looked like it was a hundred years old. She remembered in a flash that her mom had told her that Mr. Richardson had just celebrated his centennial birthday. And then the curse had drained his life force—she was sure of it. Maybe he hadn't had much life left, but every last bit was gone now. If she and Martin couldn't heal the tree, someone else would be next. Mrs. Quillen—or anyone, really. Her mom. No one was safe.

She shuddered and cracked open the book, turning to the four-page spread devoted to the football team and its glorious championship—the golden era, before curses. Before Jake stole everything. And there he was. Despite the shoulder pads, he looked slimmer, his jawline chiseled. He had tucked his helmet under his arm and thrown his big head back, laughing. In black and white, his hair appeared dark and thick, although Hannah guessed it was even redder than it was now, when the white hairs at the temples diluted the color to rusty peach.

She picked up her phone to check the time—she didn't have time to read the whole article, even if she had wanted to read about the football heroics of her number-one enemy. The thing was, in the old pictures, he didn't look evil. He didn't even look like the bloated, pompous bully who bossed Nick and A.J. around. Someone who stole life—that was the same as being a murderer. Back then, he looked like he'd be one of their friends. Maybe even one of *her* friends—one of the boys she'd kick a soccer ball around with. Or used to, before she started spending so much time with Martin and the tree.

She'd even been neglecting Waverly. Hannah realized how glad she was to be working with Martin—they were both excited about the tree. When she was with Waverly, one of them always had to convince the other to take part in anything, whether soccer or the remedial course in Barbies Waverly had given her back in second grade.

Hannah flipped to her text messages—nothing new, thank goodness. Waverly had listened. Then Hannah read the tree's old text message again.

Hurry. Time is running out.

She had known the message was from the tree from the beginning. The phone didn't list a number, but the words came from somewhere. She hit reply, then typed.

Hang on. We won't let you down. We'll stop this.

She waited for an answer, but the phone was quiet. Then a noise sounded in the wall behind her head.

Scritch scratch. Scritch scratch. Scritch scratch. The hemlock branches scraped the house, despite the windless night. There was her answer.

The Spirit Tree had heard her.

25

Libby's Surprise

Martin sat stonily while Aunt Michelle ranted. He was inconsiderate. He looked like some kind of low-class drug addict in his raggedy black T-shirt. He didn't know how to appreciate that Aunt Michelle was doing something nice for him far beyond the call of duty. He was just like his mother. Worse—like his deadbeat father. He would never learn to be successful until he understood how to treat a mentor.

The lecture began as soon as he opened the car's front door and squeezed onto the four inches of seat not occupied by Aunt Michelle's giant handbag, laptop case, and that stupid striped tote filled with designer garden tools. Martin rolled his eyes at the color-matched handles, then noticed some bark stuck in the blade of a pink electric saw, no bigger than the electric knife Abuelita had used to carve roast pork a million years ago. In fact, most of the tools looked like they'd actually been used. *Weird*, he thought. Suddenly Aunt Michelle was out pruning her own shrubs and pulling weeds. She usually never lifted a finger around the yard except to call the landscapers.

Aunt Michelle's complaints continued all through the drive, and ended only when he shut the door mid-nag when they arrived at the Greater Brynwood Community Center.

He heard Ms. Stemmler's throaty voice echoing through the open windows. Score! The meeting had already begun— he'd missed part of it. Plus, he didn't have to chat up Libby one on one while they waited for class to start. She was bad enough during school, but at Junior JET she seemed to try to sound as much like a junior executive as possible. That is, boring.

"Mr. Cruz," Ms. Stemmler said, when he peeked around the door, "how shrewd of you to make a dramatic entrance." Every eye drilled into him. "Often the most powerful people arrive last for any meeting. Let the little people wait." Ms. Stemmler pleated the creases around her mouth in a tight-lipped smile. "Have a seat while I continue my lecture on *Avaritia.*"

Martin slipped into the empty seat next to Libby, grateful that he didn't have to search around for a seat.

"*Avaritia* is a Latin word often translated as greed. We don't like that word quite as much, although Gordon Gekko popularized it for a while." Ms. Stemmler sniggered. No one picked up the reference to the movie *Wall Street*, so she said, "Greed is good." Libby wrote the three words down. "Junior Junior Executives don't believe that." Libby crossed the line out. "We just believe that greed can motivate us to acquire things that are good."

Martin looked around—every boy was wearing a suit, a sport coat, or at least a blue dress shirt. The girls looked like TV reporters. And they seemed to be paying attention to this crap. Were they already brainwashed?

"But let's not call it greed," Ms. Stemmler continued. "We prefer the English cognate—avarice. It sounds more refined. Or call it avidity. Whatever you call it, you will never succeed unless you want more than you have. But if you want more, you will get it. All you need to do is ask, and the universe will answer."

So, if Martin asked never to attend another one of these meetings, would the universe convince Aunt Michelle? Because he sure didn't want to be a Junior Junior Executive. He'd rather be a Junior Girl Scout. Join the Junior League. Attend a Junior Jamboree. Eat a Coffeecake Junior. Freshen up with a Junior Mint.

Martin had blocked out the lecture pretty well at this point. Ms. Stemmler might have called it daydreaming, but he preferred to think of it as an impenetrable Marlician dissociative mind shield. Thus, Martin was surprised when the hour (minus the first ten minutes) ended with a screech of chairs on the speckled tiles as all the blue suits stood up. Libby leaned in toward him.

Uh-oh, he thought. *Here comes the small talk.*

"I have a surprise for you," she said, her dark eyes gleaming.

He was actually surprised. "For me?"

"Yes, it's about that old Spirit Tree thing you've been working on."

"What about it?"

"I can't tell you. It would ruin the surprise. But Waverly and I have a new community history project." She paused, as if Martin was supposed to beg her to tell him what it was. When he didn't, she said, "And we're going to reveal it at the big game on Saturday."

Martin's brief feeling of flattery dissolved into dread. "What game?"

She tossed her black hair and laughed as if he were the cutest thing. "I keep forgetting you're new in town. It feels like I've known you forever."

"So, what game?"

"Lower Brynwood against Radnor. Aren't you going to the football game with Hannah?"

Martin had a thousand more questions for her, but Aunt Michelle appeared in the doorway, wearing an icy smile. She'd drag him out by his ear if he didn't leave immediately. Making the little people wait was one thing, but he didn't dare try it on Aunt Michelle.

Tonight, Junior JET; this weekend, high-school football. He'd never considered going to a game before, but now he wouldn't miss it.

On Friday Mr. Michaelson gave the class a free period to work as teams on the community history project, and Martin couldn't wait to tell Hannah about Libby's so-called surprise.

"I know all about it," she said, glancing over at Libby and Waverly, who were absorbed in conversation.

"Then what's the surprise?" Martin asked.

"I don't know that part. Just that there is a surprise."

"I have a bad feeling about this."

"Waverly said we'd like it."

Waverly and Libby giggled when they caught him looking at them. Martin was not reassured. "How would Waverly know what I like?"

"She knows me," Hannah said, then chewed the corner of her mouth.

"Does she? You told her how we talk to magical trees and try to break curses?"

"When you put it that way, it sounds silly," she said. "No one normal believes in magic."

"Not even you?"

"I don't need to. Because it's not magic—it's science." Hannah pulled out her notebook and flipped to the back section. "While you were playing your dragon computer games and hanging with Libby, I was doing research. Look."

Martin read the neat scientific timeline that Hannah had printed. He snorted. "Where did you get all this? Don't tell me it was the Internet."

Hannah grabbed the notebook back. "Some of it was. That doesn't mean it's not true."

"You might as well admit that it's magic. Jenna called it pseudoscience—a bunch of crackpots talking to plants. Otherwise these scientists would be in our textbooks."

"Charles Darwin is. See? His last book was about how plants communicate. He wasn't a crackpot."

Martin looked at the timeline—*The Power of Movement in Plants*. "Never heard of it. Probably everyone thought he went senile in his old age. Man descended from monkeys— sure, makes sense. But plants that move? Got to be soft in the head." *Like us*, he thought. "And what about these other guys?"

"Well, not all of their experiments were repeated successfully," Hannah said, flipping back to the page with the transcribed carvings. "Science *is* supposed to be repeatable."

"Aha." Martin couldn't help teasing her.

"But maybe the other scientists didn't do it right. Maybe to communicate with a plant, you need very special conditions—an old tree, the right thunderstorm."

Martin felt himself getting dragged in by her reasoning. "Maybe a plant with something important to say."

"Yeah! And the right people paying attention. Being a scientist means that you open your mind to what you observe." She flipped her notebook to the page with the transcribed messages. "And my mind is blown wide open. I *know* that tree texted us. Maybe you'd rather believe we're living in *Dragon Era*. I say there's science behind it. What's the difference, if we're both trying to do the same thing?"

Martin threw his arms up. If she wanted to believe there was a logical explanation to this mess, she could.

"This timeline is just the start of it," Hannah said. She launched into a description of Jake's connections to the tree—the football team, the carvings with his name, the beech leaf in his company logo, his plan to cut the tree down. How Jake had cursed the Spirit Tree so that he—and his dumb football team and his stupid landscape company—could benefit. Martin felt himself getting angry.

"That guy gave me the creeps the first time I saw him," he said, a bit too loud. Waverly and Libby glanced up from their project, whispered something and giggled again.

Hannah shrugged her shoulders at them. Then she leaned in toward Martin, her voice low. "So you agree that Jake is the bad one the tree told us about," she said.

"I don't doubt that he's *a* bad one. Anybody can see that," Martin said. "But is he *the* bad one? If he set the curse, why? Isn't he one of those hooray-for-everything-Lo-B types?"

"Maybe he didn't know what he was doing when he cursed. Or maybe he didn't realize that one person's gain is another's loss. And—whammo—disaster. When you do bad things, you don't always get what you expect."

"Same as when you do good things," he said, doodling the bare silhouette of the Spirit Tree on his notebook. He knew the shape by heart.

"So? It's better to do good things. It's not enough to hope. We have to try." She grabbed the pencil out of his hand so he had no choice but to look at her. "Did you know that Jake was quarterback of the Lo-B Squirrels the last time they won the championship? Heck, it was the last time the team had a winning season, period. Jake never lets Nick and A.J. forget it."

"You're saying he started the curse to win the championship, and ended up draining all the luck from Lower Brynwood?"

"I don't know." She shrugged. "Maybe it's like the law of conservation of energy. Like luck is a kind of energy—it can't be created or destroyed. It's science. For one person to gain it, it has to come from somewhere."

"Luck isn't energy," Martin said.

"Isn't it?" She looked at him with her stormy gray eyes. "You know how the tree got struck by lightning?"

"I was there."

"Maybe the tree is kind of like a lightning rod for, I don't know, luck or karma—whatever it is that's gone missing from Lower Brynwood."

"Life force," Martin whispered, thinking of how power was measured in the *Dragon Era* game.

"That's it. Life force. It's not just jobs and sports victories that disappeared from town. Except for Jenna's yard and those old woods, nothing grows here anymore—not lawns, not tomatoes, not African violets—unless Laughlin Landscaping has something to do with it. The town's dying, and Jake's the only one who benefits by picking up dead tree branches and dousing grass with chemicals. The only green spots in town are your aunt's lawn and the football field…" Hannah trailed off, studying the bare skeleton of the tree Martin had drawn.

"Do you remember when Chase got hurt during the football game?" she asked, her eyebrows furrowed again. He nodded. "The grass where he fell turned brown, like all of the life had been drained out of it."

"The tree's dying because of a curse," Martin said. "Now Jake is going to finish the job with a chainsaw."

"It's not just the tree, Martin. I think the bad one is sucking the life out of people, too."

Martin thought of the coffin holding the empty husk that had looked like his grandmother. He remembered flag-draped coffins at the Army base, too—how everyone fell silent when someone's husband, mother, son, aunt, or friend came home as a thing, not a person. The world stopped for a moment, and he felt how fragile life was. His life with his mother. Her life in a hostile country. Even the tree.

Martin began penciling leaves onto his drawing. The Spirit Tree was still alive. And he was going to make sure it stayed that way.

26

Big Game

Hannah felt as if she were walking into the stadium for the first time. Everything looked sharper, and not just because this was a Saturday afternoon game in bright sunshine instead of under Friday night lights. She noticed more because she was with Martin. She heard every note the band played, every shout rising above the general din, even smelled the scent of rubbery hotdogs coming from the snack stand, because she knew Martin hadn't been here before.

She'd had to talk him into coming, but she suspected his reluctance was a show of principle, a little protest against organized sports. Because he had to be dying to know what Libby and Waverly had planned, just like she was.

Hannah scanned the stands, but she didn't spot them. Then again, the stands were more full than usual—a sea of red, partly because fans of the Radnor Red Raiders spilled out of the visitor grandstand and into Lower Brynwood's. But there were more Lo-B fans than usual, too. Something was happening today, and it seemed like everyone was waiting for it, not just her and Martin.

Lunch the day before had been tense. Martin and Hannah tried to pump Waverly and Libby for information about whatever surprise they had planned, but the gossip sisters had turned close-mouthed. Libby acted triumphant, but Waverly was more tentative, and that made Hannah nervous. The two of them had never kept secrets from each other before, but Hannah had to admit that she had started it. She had introduced the space between them, allowing Libby to squeeze her way into the gap. Libby had mighty sharp elbows.

Hannah headed for her usual spot near the thirty-yard line, but Martin put a hand on her shoulder. She shrugged off his touch, as if it were electric. She thought of how silly they must look together, Nick Vaughan's gawky little sister with this curly-haired boy, half a head shorter and twenty pounds skinnier. Did it look like they were on a date? She felt a flutter in her chest, and she wasn't sure what it meant.

"Let's sit here," Martin said, pointing at the end of the bleachers by the entrance.

"I always sit near the middle," she said. "We can see the game better."

"We can see the field fine from here, and nobody can come in or out without us seeing them first."

They climbed to the highest bench, which gave them a view of the pothole-pocked parking lot. Plus, the top row was the only one not covered in muddy footprints.

"Look," Martin said, "you can see through the trees now." He pointed to Jenna's house.

The cottage's peaked roof and ornate chimney poked through the low trees. The brush had thinned enough that Hannah caught a glimpse of laundry on the line.

She turned back to the stadium, where Rocky, the Lower Brynwood mascot, wandered in the stands, shaking the hands of children with his furry black mitts. Up in the top row, Hannah was grateful to be out of his range. The black squirrel costume looked mangy and worn even from here, suspiciously resembling a discarded Chip costume (or maybe it was Dale) that had been spray-painted black.

Hannah saw A.J. with his buddies, then located her parents. She'd recognize the backs of their heads anywhere—her mom's short blonde hair, her father's pink scalp reflecting through his thinning hair under the early-autumn sun. There was still no sign of Waverly and Libby.

The marching band traced figures on the field, the flag team waving banners that looked heavy enough to tip them over as they gyrated to their well-worn approximations of "Louie, Louie," then "Hey Ya." And was that a Lady Gaga song in the rotation? Hannah winced at a sour note. The band needed more practice on that one.

But something else was new. A microphone stood on a small dais on the sidelines. An announcer came on as the band stood at attention.

"Ladies and gentlemen, Assistant Coach Jake Laughlin, member of the Lower Brynwood Hall of Fame and former captain of the State Champion Black Squirrels!"

Jake strode out onto the field and climbed onto the dais. He was wearing a suit instead of his usual polo shirt. Hannah and Martin exchanged worried looks. If Jake was involved, this couldn't be good.

The Black Squirrels cheerleaders filed out behind the platform, shaking red and black pompoms under their chins. Hannah's stomach felt like one of those pompoms.

Jake pulled the microphone off the stand and tapped it once, the note reverberating through the stadium. He began. "Good evening, students, teachers, parents, friends, and guests. This is the sixty-fifth meeting of the Lower Brynwood Black Squirrels and the Radnor Red Raiders in Lower Brynwood Memorial Stadium." He paused awkwardly, as if he had rehearsed. "I hope it will be the last."

The buzz of the crowd silenced for a moment, and then resumed louder than before. *The last?* Did he just say what they thought they heard?

"This will be the last meeting in this facility, because by this time next year, a new stadium will have risen in its place!" Jake glanced at the notecards in his hand, fumbling with his speech. "The school board and superintendent have already made a bond resolution, and I've been chosen as the chairman to raise ten million dollars to make it possible. You know we need a new scoreboard." He pointed to the dead hulk of the old one, black and burnt beyond the end zone. "That's only the beginning. The aluminum bleachers will be replaced with concrete. New locker rooms will support the athletic teams. And most importantly, the grass field will be replaced with artificial turf."

He paused again, and the cheerleaders lifted their pompoms above their heads as a cheer rose up like thunder. "We've already lined up corporate sponsors, starting with Horizon Network Communications. But this is a big project, and we need the whole community to make it happen. You've all heard of the Spirit Tree."

Hannah froze, and Martin clutched her arm. She was too stunned to shake him off.

"The Spirit Tree has been a symbol of Lower Brynwood pride for generations. Now, like this stadium, it's at the end of its life," Jake said, reading straight from the notecards now. "Fittingly, the tree will be honored in the first fundraiser to support the stadium. Next week, I personally, as owner of Laughlin Landscaping and Tree Care, will donate my services to cut down the Spirit Tree in an appreciation ceremony. Then, the tree will be sectioned and varnished so that the carvings are preserved. One section will be enshrined in a time capsule set in the stadium foundation. The remaining sections will be auctioned off for use as coffee tables, wall hangings, or trophies. All money raised will go toward the new stadium."

The crowd roared louder, but Hannah felt herself trembling. It was monstrous—killing the Spirit Tree, chopping it to bits, and selling the pieces as souvenirs. The stadium wouldn't hold a time capsule—it would hold a tomb. That majestic tree—older than the town itself—would be murdered to buy concrete and plastic grass. She felt her eyes fill with tears. Martin gripped her arm, hard enough now that it hurt. She put her hand on his, which loosened but didn't move.

Jake quieted the crowd again. "Souvenirs from the tree start at twenty-dollar personal donations and go right up to a corporate platinum level, which buys a tree section big enough for a lobby showpiece. Sales will begin at halftime by the snack bar."

He gestured toward a red-draped table, which had materialized as he spoke.

Libby and Waverly preened behind the table, waving to the crowd along with the members of the high-school Spirit Club. Their new project was selling the Spirit Tree.

Hannah felt sick. Waverly and Libby looked like little Spirit Club mascots, so proud to be part of the tree's destruction. Hannah's stomach lurched, and she wondered if she could throw up off the top of the grandstand without hitting anyone below.

Then Waverly caught her eye and grinned even more widely, signaling to Hannah with both hands. Hannah could only imagine the grim look on her own face, but when Waverly saw it, her smile vanished. Well, what did she expect? Did she really think Hannah would flash a big thumbs-up?

Jake saluted the crowd by holding up both hands, one of them with only two fingers raised. V for victory, Hannah guessed, something Jake had little experience with since his own high-school days. He walked off the field as the two best cheerleaders cartwheeled behind him, while the others punched the air with their pompoms.

Hannah hardly noticed the announcer introducing the teams until Head Coach Schmidt jogged out, pumping his fist, his belly and neck flab in full motion. Clearly he didn't want to be overshadowed by his assistant Jake, who retook the field modestly, clapping for his boss but looking like an Academy Award winner applauding the losing nominees.

Nick ran out last, his hair shining yellow in the light. Hannah's heart flipped. No matter what Jake threatened to do, she had to root for Nick. She wanted Lower Brynwood to win. The town and the Spirit Tree had suffered together because of the curse, and she and Martin were going to stop it.

Nick couldn't have known any of this. The game began, and Nick was on fire, passing bullets, marshaling the offense. Hannah knew that feeling. He was spurred by the crowd's energy, by the sea of red jerseys and hats (even if some of them were worn by their rivals), the thought that his senior season would be a fitting finale for the stadium.

By the end of the first quarter, Nick had one hundred fifteen yards passing on eight completions to six receivers, including a twenty-five-yard touchdown pass. Hannah had told her brother earlier, "You throw enough touchdowns, you've got to win some football games." She meant he needed to do his own job, and everything else would sort itself out. And at least in the game, it was happening. The Lower Brynwood Black Squirrels led, twenty-one to three.

The offense squared off at the line of scrimmage, Nick's black helmet looming above the shoulder pads of his teammates. Lo-B threatened to score again, just inside the Radnor twenty-yard line. The roar of the crowd really sounded like thunder now. Nick took the snap, dropped back, and pumped his arm, looking for a receiver. A Radnor tackle broke through the line. Nick scrambled, then the tackle was on him, and three more big bodies piled on.

When the red shirts peeled off, Nick didn't get up. Hannah's stomach seized again, and she felt as if she would fall.

The trainers jogged out, but this time they followed Head Coach Schmidt, his face red and cheeks puffy. Hannah felt as if she was watching a replay of the scene when Chase was injured, except that this time more was at stake. This time, the injured player was her brother. The tears that had threatened when Jake announced the tree's fate had dried up, and Hannah felt a cold wind blow over the wide parking lot.

Head Coach Schmidt's gravely voice rose above the crowd. "Get up, get up, get up, you pansy!"

Then Hannah heard an odd, strangled cry within the circle of players, followed by a panicked scuffle, but she couldn't see beyond the solid wall of shoulder pads. *That yell didn't come from Nick.* At first the thought relieved her, and then she was even more worried. What was happening?

After a few minutes, EMTs brought out a stretcher, staggering under its weight. The bulky figure on the pallet wasn't Nick. It was Head Coach Schmidt, clutching his chest. The EMTs loaded him into the ambulance, turned on the lights, rolled across the field, and burned out of the parking lot. A trainer and Jake each put an arm around Nick, helping him to the bench. The players followed as a grim entourage. A trainer flashed a light in Nick's eyes, and Nick tried to wave him off.

Hannah clambered down the bleachers, pressing her way to the edge of the track. She put one hand on Martin's shoulder to balance as she stood on her tiptoes, but she could see less than before. After a few agonizing moments, A.J. found her. He wrapped his arms around her, and she felt very small, leaning against her brother as he filled her in on what had happened.

Head Coach Schmidt had probably had a heart attack, and Nick was out with a suspected concussion. Their parents would accompany him to the hospital for evaluation.

"Nick got his bell rung pretty good," A.J. said, keeping an arm around Hannah's shoulder. She realized she must look pretty shaken. "They take these things seriously these days, but it's just part of the game. Nothing worse than the hits I took to the head, and I'm still a super genius."

She smiled wanly.

"I'll take you home," he said. "Martin, too."

Hannah let A.J. steer her toward the players' entrance. The crowd opened up for him, and Hannah felt herself being eyed by them. She lifted her head so her ponytail swung behind, grateful that they wouldn't have to walk by Waverly and Libby. Then she heard the crowd shout at a completed pass, and took a last look at the field. The game continued under Assistant Coach Jake Laughlin and the backup quarterback, as if Nick had never been there.

But not exactly. Hannah stared at the turf. In the middle of field were two more dead brown patches. And the grass under Jake's feet glowed greener than before.

Light flared behind him, bright as lightning. The broken scoreboard had blazed to life, every bulb burning. No one but Hannah seemed to notice, not even Martin. She craned her neck to look behind her, stumbling as A.J. guided her forward. The scoreboard clock raced backwards, a hundred times faster than real time, and Hannah felt panic rising in her throat as the numbers ticked away. The clock counted down to zero, then blinked out.

The scoreboard was black and silent, the traces etched on Hannah's retinas the only sign that it had ever been lit. Time was running out. The message was clear, but was it a warning or a threat? Was there even a difference? Hannah and Martin were failing. They had already failed Nick.

Later at home, Hannah heard that the Black Squirrels had won—their first win in two seasons, and their first defeat of Radnor since Jake had been the captain.

27

Wrong Man

Hannah didn't talk much on the ride home, and Martin couldn't blame her. The tree was going to be dismembered and sold off as trophies. Waverly had gone over to the dark side, Nick had gotten hurt, and Jake Laughlin was a part of it.

Still, Martin couldn't blame A.J. for trying to lighten the mood—he seemed like a pretty good guy. Plus, it was clear he hated Jake just as much as they did—a big plus in his favor.

"I don't know how Jake did it," A.J. said. "Not about how the stadium deal happened—we've needed a new one for the past fifteen years. You saw what happened to that old scoreboard." Hannah lifted her head for a moment, then put it down. "The field is worse. It's a miracle anybody can rush five yards without turning an ankle. And Nick's concussion? No surprise—I swear there's cement under that grass. You wouldn't believe the bruises we logged, even during no-contact drills."

"So? What's so amazing about that?" Martin said, interrupting since Hannah clearly wasn't going to say anything. "Jake the Snake—isn't that what the guys used to call him back in the day? So he's slimy. Big surprise."

"Snakes aren't really slimy," Hannah said without looking up.

"Whatever," A.J. said. "They called him that because he could slip a tackle like he had no bones. Plus, it rhymed." He shrugged.

"Snakes are vertebrates. They have bones," said Hannah.

"Thanks, Dr. Doolittle," A.J. said, giving his sister a shove with his elbow. "But I'm not surprised he's underhanded. I'm shocked 'cause I would've thought something this big was way beyond him."

"You mean beneath him," Hannah said. She sounded as if she wanted to say more, and Martin worried that she'd spill the whole Spirit Tree story.

A.J. shook his head. "Nah. He's pretty greedy. I can believe he'd chop up the tree to make a few bucks—he cuts corners and pads invoices whenever he gets a chance. But how did he get the superintendent, much less Head Coach Schmidt, to let *him* make that announcement?"

"What do you mean?" Martin asked.

"Dad works for the township," A.J. said. "You should hear the stories he tells. But if there's one thing he taught us, it's that the guys at the top take credit for anything good and lay blame for anything bad."

"Mud flows downhill," Martin said. It was just like his mom always said.

"You got it. But announcing a new stadium at a football game? How did some nobody landscaper-slash-assistant-coach get that task? Why didn't someone else take the mic?"

"Maybe Jake had the best suit," Martin said, joking. He looked at Hannah, hoping she would smile, but she had closed her eyes and showed no sign that she'd heard him. "At Junior Junior Executives of Tomorrow, they say to dress for the job you want, not the job you have."

"Is that right?" A.J. said. "I wonder how I'd look mowing lawns in a spacesuit. I used to want to be an astronaut."

Hannah spoke up, sounding annoyed. "Maybe they picked Jake to be symbolic. I'm surprised he didn't come out wearing football gear—he always wants everyone to know that he was the last quarterback to win a state championship for Lo-B."

A.J. laughed. "Well, *pro* quarterback was the job he wanted back then. Me, too, if I'm honest, but it didn't work out for either of us. Neither of us even played college ball."

"If he was so good his senior year, why not?" Martin said. A.J. took his eyes off the road to shoot Martin a wrathful look. "I'm sure you were good, too," he added quickly.

"I was good. But you're wrong about one thing. Neither Jake nor I won a single game our senior year, but at least I got to play."

"Wait a minute," Martin said, confused. "How'd he win the championship if he didn't play?"

"The championship was his junior year. To hear him tell it, college scouts were all over him during senior pre-season. Wouldn't leave him alone—Penn State, Ohio State, Notre Dame. Then old Jake tore his ACL during his senior home opener. Never got to play again—no more wins, no scholarship. No college, either. He's been cutting lawns ever since, and hating every minute of it."

Hannah said in a hoarse whisper, "What year was that?"

"He was the class of '90, so the fall season was actually 1989. The championship was '88, then the next year Lower Brynwood lost every game. Hasn't had a winning season since."

Hannah and Martin exchanged wide-eyed looks. The curse began in 1989. That meant Jake the Snake Laughlin was injured just days after the first Spirit Tree ceremony. He hadn't benefited at all—he was one of the first victims. Whether the bad one had set the curse for revenge or to gain, Jake didn't fit. He might be a bad guy, all right, but he wasn't the person they were looking for.

Martin looked out the window at the trees that lined the streets. The skeletal black shapes rushed by. Hannah and Martin were nearly out of time, and whoever had cursed the Spirit Tree was still out there.

Hannah's brother probably thought she'd cry as soon as she shut her attic door, but she felt more like yelling. She might not know how to fix her hair or pick out shoes, but her brothers had always teased her for acting like a girl— emotional, vain. Silly. And sure, she wore lip gloss and liked furry little animals, but she had always prided herself on being logical. More logical than Nick and A.J., anyway.

But when it came to the Spirit Tree, she had completely lost it. But how could a person think logically when she was talking to a tree? Her mind really had been blown. No matter how much she tried to find scientific justification, she just had to accept what her senses told her and go along. And Martin might think they were living in *Dragon Era* Marlicia, but he was the one that kept trying to pull her back from jumping from one half-baked assumption to another.

But that was no excuse for other lapses. It was written right in the notebook: *Forever young, 9/15/89*. How could she forget that school sessions span two calendar years? So a curse that started in the fall of 1989 would affect the graduating class of 1990, not the class of 1989.

She restrained herself from throwing Dr. Wiggins's yearbook across the room. She would hate to disappoint him by destroying his book in a tantrum.

Speaking of disappointing, Waverly had sure done it. Disappointment was too weak a word—betrayal was more like it. She and Libby were working with Jake. While he might not have actually cursed the Spirit Tree, now he was trying to usher in its doom, and for what? Money. Filthy money. Greed.

She picked up her phone—five messages from Waverly. She couldn't bring herself to read them, but she didn't delete them, either. Instead, she reread the message from her parents. Her mom had texted that Nick was alert and seemed fine, but that the hospital was keeping him overnight for observation. The Vaughan parents were sleeping over, too.

She had run downstairs and nearly hugged A.J. out of relief, but A.J. had brushed her off.

"Of course Nick will be okay, Banana," he said. "The real question is whether the coach will let him start after a head injury. If he doesn't play, he can kiss that scholarship goodbye."

She remembered Head Coach Schmidt's heart attack, which hadn't affected her nearly as much as what was happening with Nick, the tree, or even Waverly. She should have asked how he was, but instead she said, "Coach Schmidt? Is he going to be back in action so soon?"

"Not Coach Schmidt. He's alive and stable for now, but he's not going to be coaching for a while. I meant Coach Laughlin," A.J. said miserably. "Good old Jakey is the acting head coach now. I guess he got the job he wanted, after all. Must have been the suit."

Hannah opened the yearbook and flipped to the junior class. There was young Jake Laughlin—so smug, like he ruled the universe. He had no idea all his plans were going to be dust in a few months.

Nick had a chance to win this season. Heck, he hadn't finished the game tonight, but his arm had earned those touchdowns. He deserved the credit for the win. But would Jake let history repeat itself and keep Nick off the squad, or would he let him play and win? She wasn't sure which would be better. Nick would want to play. But why bother going to college if he ended up brain-damaged to get there? The price was too high.

The landline rang. Hannah raced to the phone next to the computer, but paused before answering—Waverly? Bad news from Mom?

"Are you all right?" Martin didn't identify himself, but Hannah would recognize his voice anywhere, even though he had never called her before. She felt a quiver at the back of her throat and realized how glad she was to hear from him.

"Been better," she said. "But Nick's doing okay. And the coach is probably going to be all right, too."

"But not the Spirit Tree."

"No. Martin, what are we going to do? We've been chasing another dead end." She picked up a pen and doodled on a crumpled piece of paper on the counter.

"One thing I learned from *Dragon Era* is that when you realize you're in a blind alley, the best thing to do is turn around and retrace your steps," said Martin. "Go back to where you started."

"What are you talking about?"

"Didn't you say once we had a trunk full of clues? There are dozens of other carvings. It's time we started analyzing them all."

"I don't know." She scribbled six sigmas, then crossed them out. They'd gotten her nowhere. "It's too late for you to come over, and I'm too worn out to think straight."

"I didn't mean, like, right now. Tomorrow will be fine."

"Oh," Hannah said. She was even more tired than she thought. "Okay, I'll meet you at your house after church—say, 1:30?"

She hung up the phone and thought about what Martin had said.

Go back to where you started.

She looked at the crumpled paper in her hand. It was a street map of Lower Brynwood, marked up with little Xs in different colors. Stamped in the corner: Compliments of Laughlin Landscaping and Tree Care.

"Hey, A.J., is this map yours?" she called to her brother, flopped in front of the TV.

"It was. It's pretty well done for at this point," he said, keeping his eyes on the sports highlights. "So am I."

"I can see that. What do these Xs mean?"

"Locations of fallen trees I had to clean up this week—trees don't have street addresses, so I marked up the map to plan my route. You can keep it—I used a different color each day, but I'm out of colors. I'll pick up a new map tomorrow when I get new marching orders from the boss."

Climbing the steps to her room, Hannah smoothed the map out as best she could. *Go back to where you started.* Hannah turned Martin's words over in her head. As soon as she had fixated on Jake, she'd thrown all the other clues out the window. And now they had to throw out the idea of Jake as a suspect. But what if he *was* part of it? When the tree was cursed in 1989, Jake had suffered as much as anyone. But now that it was dying, he was benefiting. He was the head of the fundraising committee. He had gotten the head-coach job, at least for now. His company was in line for a high-profile job executing and butchering the Spirit Tree, and Hannah didn't doubt that he'd bid on the landscaping for the new stadium.

There was some connection they were missing, and they'd figure it out. She located Brynwood Park and drew a little picture of the Spirit Tree right about where it would be located—where it all started.

She pulled out her phone. Another two messages from Waverly. She sighed. She had to respond. Without reading the messages, she typed her own: NICK OK. TALK 2MORROW.

Phone tag complete. Now Waverly's it, she thought. She had to admit that her BFF was right about one thing—sending a text was easier than talking sometimes.

Other times it was the only way.

Hannah sent another text, closing her eyes to try to feel the radio emanations beaming through the ether. A message to the Spirit Tree.

Still trying. Hang on a little longer.

She waited, hoping for a response, or at least a scratch on the wall relayed by the hemlock outside her room. Nothing. Vincent Vaughan Gogh poked his lopsided head up the steps. Scooping up the cat, she walked to the cracked dormer window. The hemlock branches that had once scraped the house lay scattered on the ground beneath the window. Dead wood. This old hemlock tree was dying, catching up to everything else in Lower Brynwood. Lower Deadwood, as Martin called it. Now the sky showed through its bare branches, and a harvest moon hung low in the red glow of the nearby city. Amid the blaze of the corner streetlights, Lower Brynwood at night was nearly as bright as a stormy day. A cloud passed before the moon. In the half-darkness, Hannah saw was she was looking for.

There, just about where the Spirit Tree would be, a faint column of light projected onto the dome of sky. It could have been a searchlight, advertising the opening of a distant supermarket opening or car dealership, but Hannah knew it wasn't.

The beam came from the tree, energy streaming up and disappearing into the clouds. It wavered for a moment, and Hannah couldn't tell if it grew brighter or dimmer, or even if it was flashing, signaling in a code she couldn't understand. But the light was real. It was there.

Then the cloud moved, and the column of brightness seemed to disappear, camouflaged once again in the glare of light pollution.

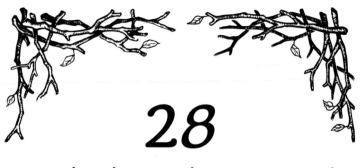

28

Back Where They Started

Hannah showed up on the doorstep wearing running shorts and sneakers.

"You wore that to church?" Martin asked. If his mom were there she'd never let him get away with that outfit at Sunday Mass. But she wasn't, so he was dressed almost exactly like Hannah, except that he wasn't wearing a sports bra. He reddened at the thought.

"No church. Nick got discharged from the hospital an hour ago," she said, grinning.

"Awesome. He's okay?"

"Okay enough to come home and order us around. Okay enough to play? I don't know. He has a minor concussion."

"Brain injuries are no joke," Martin said, thinking of some of his mom's friends who had come back from tours of duty with headaches, memory loss, or just plain different.

"I have to be back in time for the evening church service, though. We have to give thanks and all." She bent to retie her sneakers, and Martin averted his eyes from her red tank. "You and I'd better get going."

"Get going? Where?" he asked. She was confusing him more than usual.

"You said last night we should go back to where we started," Hannah said, standing with a shrug and adjusting a frayed backpack on her shoulders. "We started at the tree."

He looked around. "So, where's your bike?"

"Since your mom's not here and your iPod is one hundred percent broken, I figured you needed a real training partner. I'll run."

"If you can keep up." Martin sprinted off, and she caught him quickly. He slowed to a normal pace, maybe a touch faster than normal. She was taller than he was, but their strides matched well. He found himself more conscious of his own breathing with her exhaling beside him. They didn't talk, and he didn't mind. When they moved through the trail in the woods, Hannah swiveled her head around, looking over her shoulder.

"Do you hear that?" she asked.

"What?"

"I don't know—footsteps. Like someone is running with is."

He listened, and he heard it, too. The noise wasn't on the ground—it flew through the trees, a rustle in the yellowing underbrush, a crackle in the treetops, a snap of twigs, a sound as if a team of very large squirrels were running along the branches in step with them. But he saw nothing. The noise came from the woods themselves, a signal relayed by the trees. Martin had heard that sound before.

"The Spirit Tree knows we're coming," he said.

"Of course. I told it we'd be here. But I guess that wasn't really necessary."

The two slowed to a walk as they approached the Spirit Tree. Martin reached out his hand to touch the trunk; so did Hannah. "We're here," she said.

Damp tendrils had escaped her ponytail, and Martin could see her pulse trembling in the hollow between her neck and her collarbone.

"What did you want to do here?" Martin asked, flapping his wet T-shirt to cool down. She had seemed so sure of their mission that he had followed without asking. "Didn't we already copy everything down from the bark?"

She nodded. "We're just visiting. We can't forget what this is about." Then she said more softly, "Did you signal me last night?"

Confused, Martin answered, "You mean, after I called you?"

"I wasn't talking to you, Martin. I was talking to the Spirit Tree."

The tree crackled like a burning log. A light flared up in the bark—the Y in Brynwood, then an E, after a pause. Then an S.

Hannah's brows knitted together. "I saw a light in the woods—I knew it was you."

The spark flowed from one letter to another, slowly now, as if it were painful. S, T, O, then the light faded out.

"Would it be easier to text on the phone?" Martin asked, not quite sure if he was talking to Hannah or the tree. His blood still hammered in his temples, but he shivered in the fall air as the sweat evaporated from his T-shirt.

Hannah's phone buzzed, vibrating in the side pocket of her bag. Martin smiled as she dug it out. The tree had heard.

STOLEN. THE BAD ONE IS STEALING IT ALL. ENERGY. LIFE.

"Is that what the curse does?" Hannah asked.

STOLEN FROM ME. STOLEN THROUGH ME.

"But what do we do?"

YOU MUST STOP IT.

Then the trunk of the tree blazed almost as brightly as the first night they saw it, when they thought the wood was burning from the inside.

HEAL ME. HEAL ALL.

"We're trying," Hannah said. "We have maybe two weeks until…" She broke off, and Martin knew she was thinking of Jake's chainsaw. The tree was dying. It probably already knew about the plan to cut it down.

"We're hurrying," Martin said.

Hurry faster.

Martin rolled his eyes. Bossy thing. He was surrounded by them.

Hannah just gave the scarred, silvery bark a pat. "We will," she said, turning to Martin. "Let's go."

His heart rate hadn't even had time to calm down and they were off. He guessed this could be considered interval training, and hoped it would make him faster. "Where are we going now?"

"We need a 1990 yearbook—Dr. Wiggins's is the wrong year," she said. "We have to cross-reference all those names on the trunk, including Jake's. We need to know who's on there, and what might have happened to them, good or bad. We should have done this two weeks ago."

Martin snapped back, "You're not blaming me for that."

"I'm not," she said, a line between her eyes. Martin found it hard to read her expression as she concentrated on breathing. They had run about two miles by that point. He was just getting warmed up, but she looked tired.

"Who has a yearbook? Don't tell me we're going to borrow Jake's."

"Nope. Time to pay a visit to our friendly neighborhood witch," Hannah said, panting a little.

"Jenna? I thought you didn't believe she was a witch."

"I don't," she said. "At this point, I wish she was. Extra magic on our side wouldn't hurt." She gave him a playful push on the shoulder, and Martin almost stumbled off the running path. He regained his footing and grinned. It really was magic if Hannah had come around to his way of thinking.

Jenna didn't look surprised to see them. She opened the oak door before Martin's knuckles hit it for a second rap.

"Did you see us coming in your crystal ball?" Hannah asked.

"What?" Jenna peered at them from beneath a broad-brimmed straw hat, looking like a pioneer woman except for her rainbow-colored rubber clogs.

"Nothing—just a joke," Martin said, nudging Hannah with the toe of his sneaker.

"Actually, I wasn't expecting you. I did wonder how things were going on your quest, but I didn't know how to contact you. I'm not even sure of your last names."

"Vaughan."

"Cruz."

"Pleased to make your acquaintance," Jenna said, pronouncing each letter clearly in that funny formal diction she used. "And I want to thank you for introducing me to the Spirit Tree—I'm confident it'll qualify as a Champion Tree. I'm not sure if we can keep it alive, but at least we'll get the chance to try. Join me in the garden—fall cleanup won't wait."

She walked out between them, pulling on a pair of green gloves. Martin and Hannah fell into step behind her.

"How do you get your garden so lush?" Hannah asked. "My mom tries to grow flowers, but everything else around here seems to be dying."

"You call it lush. Others call it overgrown. In fact, someone has been hacking away at some of my shrubs when I'm gone, and I have a feeling it's the president of the local community association. She's never been my biggest admirer," Jenna said, kneeling down to hack at a weed with a well-used hand trowel.

Martin shifted uncomfortably, thinking of the bag of used garden tools in Aunt Michelle's car. Aha. That's what they were for—vigilante gardening in the name of Brynwood Estates Community Association. She always said the power was in her hands, but he never thought she meant a power saw. Fortunately, Jenna had no idea that he was related to Michelle Medina.

He inhaled deeply, and smelled something sweet and dense in the air. He realized for the first time that the air fresheners Aunt Michelle sprayed constantly were supposed to imitate actual flowers, not just something invented in a factory. This scent was somehow simpler and more complex at the same time, and beneath the perfume he sensed something dark—musty earth, decaying leaves. Jenna's garden was real and old in a way that Aunt Michelle would never tolerate. He remembered that Hannah had told him the cottage was a gatehouse once.

"Dr. Blitzer, was this house really here when Thomas Brynwood was alive?" he asked, although he wasn't sure why.

"The cottage wasn't. It's Victorian—built when Thomas Brynwood was long buried," she said, looking up from her weeds with her sharp blue eyes. "But the estate was his once. Some of these plants might have been here. That old ash, possibly. The daffodils nestled under the ground might have been planted then, maybe a single bulb that multiplied into the huge clumps and sweeps that grow here each spring. Likely the distant ancestors of these asters bloomed then, and definitely the progenitors of the weeds I battle daily. That's one reason I love this cottage—not just the pretty gothic stonework, but the way the land is still connected to an older time."

"It's beautiful," Hannah said, touching the petals of a tall blue aster as if it might break.

"A wilder garden takes getting used to, but this is what landscape ecology is about," Jenna said. Still kneeling, she snapped off the aster and raised it to Hannah with a flourish, who smiled and tucked it behind her ear. "The beauty is the interplay of species—not just plants, but how they communicate with, harmonize with, and depend upon animals in their midst. You've met my bees, but I've identified more than three dozen animal species in here. It's their garden as well as mine—rabbits, insects, birds, bats."

"Bats?" Martin asked, involuntarily hunching his shoulders. Thank goodness it wasn't dark.

"Of course," Jenna said, the lines around her eyes crinkling into fine folds. "Maybe those little houses on the posts would seem less charming if you knew that they weren't for birds. They're bat houses."

"Bat houses. Huh," Martin said. He remembered the bees swarming over him and pictured the same scene, but with bats. Not pleasant. He made a mental note to escape before dark. "Um, we actually came for something. Could we please borrow your high-school yearbook?"

Jenna stabbed her trowel into the ground and stared at them. "My yearbook? What are you talking about?"

Martin had forgotten Jenna didn't know what they were really up to—she didn't even know he was related to Michelle Medina. He gaped, not sure what to say.

Hannah laughed a little, as if it was all a harmless misunderstanding instead of a continuing, life-or-death deception. She lifted her hand, as if to twist her earring, but touched the flower in her hair instead. "It's all part of the community history project. Remember, we're trying to find out who might have made which carving, and since it's mostly high-school kids, we thought a yearbook might have some clues."

"Ah, yes. So, you haven't found out who carved those mysterious sigmas?"

"Well, no," Hannah paused, kicking a clod of dirt with her toe. "We got sidetracked. We didn't think they were important, after all."

"If you don't know what they mean, how can you tell they're not important? You have to consider all the evidence before you dismiss it."

Hannah bit her lip, so Martin stepped in. "Do you have a yearbook? Dr. Wiggins told us you'd have one for 1990. He gave us one from 1989."

"You can't mean Mark Wiggins?" Jenna relaxed. Martin had said the right thing for once. "I haven't thought of him for years. I had such a crush on him back then—the big senior in the state science fair. He never seemed to notice me, though."

Hannah looked wistful, touching the blue flower again, then her hand dropped and she asked, "So, can we please borrow the yearbook, Dr. Blitzer?"

"Of course you can. It's not like I spend a lot of time reliving my glory days. I wish I could forget most of it. High school was so humiliating." She stood, plucked off her gloves, and dusted her hands. "Let me get the book. Just don't hold anything in it against me."

Hannah frowned as soon as she disappeared.

"I can't believe we—I—could have been so stupid," she said. "We forgot all about those dumb sigmas as soon as we focused on Jake."

"Don't worry about the leads we didn't follow. We're doing it now."

"But it could be too late," she said. "I'm the one who brought Jake into this. If I hadn't asked for his help, he never would have thought of the Spirit Tree, much less decided to chop it down for fun and profit." Hannah hunched her shoulders.

"You were trying to help." He wanted to touch her, but kept his hands by his sides.

"Some help. I'm worse than the curse," she said, her face crumpling. "Whatever we do, we can't tell Jenna what Jake's planning."

"But she said the tree's a rare specimen—maybe she could hold up his application. Your dad's trying to slow down the process, but she could stop it. She's a professor—people would listen to her."

"But *we* have to do it." Hannah's voice pitched upward. "The tree asked *us*, and if we stop Jake, Jenna will never know what he's planning. I don't want her to know that we've been lying to her."

The screen door screeched open, and Jenna held a maroon, leather-covered book beneath her arm and a glass of iced green tea in each hand.

"That was quick," Martin said, hoping she didn't notice that Hannah was upset.

"My library is well-organized," Jenna answered. "I thought you two looked thirsty."

"Thanks," said Martin, swirling the glass so the ice cubes clinked.

Hannah chugged her drink like a pro. When she had drained the glass in record time, she wiped her mouth with the back of her hand. "Thanks, Dr. Blitzer, but we really have to get going—my parents are expecting me any minute." She handed the glass back to Jenna. Martin hadn't even taken two sips.

"OK then," said Jenna, holding out a card that looked like it was made out of an old paper bag. "Here's my business card. If you let me know when you're coming, I can make pumpkin bread."

"Thanks!" Hannah slipped the card into the yearbook, zipped up her backpack, and turned to leave. Martin took one last, delicious gulp of iced tea before he gave Jenna the almost-full glass and followed Hannah as she shot off in a sprint. She was faster than he was over short distances.

"Where are we going?" he said, gasping. "Why'd we leave so fast?"

"I really have to go home," she said over her shoulder. The flower had fallen from her hair. "I'm already so late I won't be able to shower before church. My brother will wish he were back in the hospital if he has to sit next to me."

Martin would have sat next to her all day, no matter what she smelled like. He was probably pretty ripe, too, as his mom used to say. *Used to say?* The ache in his chest had nothing to do with exertion. Martin reminded himself that his mom would say the same thing if she were there. She was far away, but she was still the same mom he knew—the same quick temper, the same wicked sense of humor, the same endless energy, the same good nature that refused to see anything bad in Martin, even when it stared her in the face.

The moment he got back to Aunt Michelle's house, he looked for his mom online. Her IM account was inactive, so he sent an email.

Hi Mom. School is going as great as I expected. I think my social studies teacher Mr. Michaelson is really interested in my work. Hannah, A.J., Waverly, Libby, Jenna, Jake, and I are all working on the same project with the Spirit Tree, but we're kinda going in different directions. Ha! You know how that is. I wish you were here to get us working together. We could use a logistical expert. I've been running a lot, and Hannah is helping me train.

Well, I better take a shower now, because I have a club meeting for Junior Junior Executives of Tomorrow later. Aunt Michelle likes me to look sharp.

Stay safe.

Love, Martin

None of it was a lie. It wasn't all true, either, but that was the best that Martin could do. His mom always said his best was good enough, but he didn't think that was true, either.

Martin wondered how Aunt Michelle's Lexus managed to be simultaneously luxurious and completely uncomfortable.

Forget the fact that he had to squeeze in next to her computer stuff and some very dangerous-looking designer gardening crap—the problem was the company. He never thought he'd miss A.J.'s bumpy bench seat and horrible taste in sports radio.

At least for once he actually had something to talk about with Aunt Michelle. Might as well follow up one of those old leads. "Aunt Michelle? Have you ever heard of Six Sigma?"

"Don't tell me they're teaching you about that in Junior Junior Executives of Tomorrow," she said.

"No, no. I read something about it somewhere else," he said, hoping she wouldn't pry.

"Well, don't read any more of it. Six Sigma is outdated," she said, and Martin felt some of his discomfort easing, like air escaping from an overinflated tire. "The Happy Elf Bakery tried it, and look what happened."

"What happened?" Martin asked. "I'm not from around here."

Aunt Michelle's mouth was off and running full-speed. "The company tanked, and it was the fault of everyone who worked there. When business started going downhill, a bunch of Six Sigma consultants got the management stuck on method, science, incremental improvement, and more methods. They even came in to tell us about it in Junior Executives of Tomorrow. I was in high school, but I already knew that's not how you get things done," she said, shaking her head with a sneer. "When you want something, you don't get it with a mathematical formula. You get it by going for it—grabbing it with both hands and even taking it by force, if that's what you have to do."

"Are you still talking about business?" Martin said.

"Of course. That's how I became vice-president of Horizon Network Communications," she said, pointing at a placard on the dashboard as proof—*Reserved Executive*

Parking. "Everyone thought cell phones were a fad when I started in the mobile division, but now look at me. I started doing the job like I owned the place, and now I practically do. That's how I became president of Junior Executives of Tomorrow and co-vice president of the Spirit Club back in high school, and it's how I became the youngest-ever president of the Brynwood Estates Community Association. Nobody wanted that job until I took it. Back then, everyone thought the association was just about telling people what kind of trash cans they could have and when to put them at the curb."

"Isn't it?" Martin said. "You complain about it enough."

"So? Who wants the neighborhood to look trashy?" she snapped. "Next thing you know, the streets of Brynwood Estates will be lined with pickup trucks and broken lawn chairs, just like the hills of Lower Brynwood."

"There are worse things," Martin said. Hannah lived in the hills, and he preferred the shabby twin houses to the fancy cardboard boxes Aunt Michelle ruled over.

"But I want better," she said, cruising through a yellow traffic light. "That's why I took over the garden club from those dumpy old ladies with dirty fingernails. Power was there for the taking, and now nobody in Brynwood Estates says boo to me. Except Jenna Blitzer—she's been thumbing her nose at me for years, fighting citations, arguing in meetings in front of the whole committee. Now I'm finally going to beat her. Not by incremental change, asking her to mow her grass two inches shorter or chopping down those overgrown shrubs when she's not looking. No, the Lower Brynwood city planners just asked for my input into the new parking lot for the high-school stadium. Bigger stadium, more cars, more concrete. We'll need more land near the school, and all we have to do is seize it. Eminent domain!"

"What's that?" Martin asked. He didn't like the sound of it.

"A nice legal loophole. I love rules!" she said with the kind of enthusiasm normal people reserved for puppies or ice cream. "People like me make them, and people like her follow them."

"But I thought she didn't have to follow the community association rules."

"She has to obey this one," Aunt Michelle said. "Eminent domain means the township has the right to seize any property needed for development in the public interest. They pay the property owner, but the property owner can't refuse. Guess whose land we're going to use for the parking lot?"

Martin felt a little sick. Aunt Michelle didn't wait for him to answer.

"Jenna Blitzer's," she said, nearly singing. "That eyesore of a weed patch will be wiped from the face of the earth." She laughed. "And she doesn't even know it yet. I'd love to be the one to tell her, but apparently the town has lawyers for that."

She stopped the car in front of the community center and snapped the power locks open. "Here you are, Martin. Junior Junior Executives of Tomorrow. Have fun."

Martin was too stunned to shake off Libby's attention when she sat next to him in the meeting.

"Now we're working on the Spirit Tree together!" Libby said. "My parents are the town's lawyers, and they helped Waverly and me get on the student fundraising committee."

"We're not working together. I'm trying to save the tree, and you're trying to sell it," he said, raising his voice.

She cocked her head. "I'm preserving it, just like you are. We're saving the carvings instead of letting them rot in the woods."

"But you're killing it." Martin heard his voice crack, and Libby looked at him with pity, like he was talking about an imaginary friend.

"It's just a tree. It's not like it's a living thing," she said.

"A tree *is* a living thing."

"You know what I mean. It's not an animal. It's just wood. Wood is meant to be used—made into furniture, paper, or whatever. You should be happy they're not using the Spirit Tree as fuel for the homecoming bonfire."

"Do I look happy?" He gritted his teeth.

"No. But you know, a smile wouldn't hurt you. And before long you'll find yourself feeling better if you're looking better."

Martin inhaled, flaring his nostrils. He felt as if he was about to blow smoke out his nose and ears, and he was still fuming as Ms. Stemmler cleared her phlegmy throat to call the meeting to order. "Good evening, ladies and gentlemen," she said. "Today we're talking about a subject everyone loves—*Luxuria*. That is, luxury."

Jenna's home and garden were going to be bulldozed—cut down and trashed, just like the Spirit Tree. Martin couldn't stand to think of it, but he couldn't get it out of his head.

"If you want to be successful, you have to surround yourself with the trappings of success—an elegant home, a luxury car, designer clothes," Ms. Stemmler said. She winked, pursing her lips as if they were closed with a drawstring. "Or, if you're a kid, a super-deluxe gaming system and expensive jeans. If you look like a leader, you'll attract others—whether executives or other students—to you. And when you attract others, you attract more success. You have power to make things happen. That's the answer."

Martin covered his head with his hands. His expensive new suit and tie felt like a straitjacket. He hadn't been able to make anything happen. All this time, he'd thought he was a third-level rogue ranger, and it turned out he was an NPC—a non-player character, a dead-eyed prop in the background of the real game.

29

Walkout

Hannah didn't call Waverly back. The more time passed, the harder it was to break the silence. They hadn't spoken since school on Friday, and now it was a quarter to ten on Sunday night. Fifty-four hours had passed, but who was counting? It was almost too late—even Waverly wasn't allowed to take calls past ten on a school night.

Hannah toyed with her phone, then powered it on for the first time since Nick had come home from the hospital. It rang immediately, and she answered without looking at the number.

"Waverly?" she asked.

"No, it's me," Martin said, his voice breaking a little.

Hannah was disappointed, relieved, and excited to hear him all at once. "I'm glad you called. What's up?"

"Nothing good."

Hannah could hear a gulp on the other end.

"It's about Jenna Blitzer," Martin said.

"Don't tell me she's a suspect again."

"That's not it. My aunt told me the town is going to seize her land. They're going to pave it over for a stadium parking lot."

Hannah felt numb. "What? They can't do that."

"They can, Hannah. It's called eminent domain. The town can take her land if they say it's for the public good, and Jenna's property backs up to the football field. The stadium committee already gave the go-ahead—they just need the town lawyers, also known as Libby's parents—to condemn the property, and then it's theirs to buy. An offer she can't refuse."

That beautiful place, the only green and wild place outside Brynwood Park, was going to be destroyed, just like the tree. Fury burned through Hannah's body from the middle of her chest into her brain. "They can't do that."

"Yes, they can," Martin said. "The Lower Brynwood Planning Commission just needs a few signatures, then Jenna's garden will be asphalt."

"The Lower Brynwood Planning Commission?" said Hannah, the heat in her head cooling enough to think clearly. "Are you forgetting we have pull there? My dad will help us. He's got the Spirit Tree removal plan stalled, no matter what Jake claimed yesterday at the football game. Dad can slow down the condemnation. Maybe we can save the tree *and* Jenna's house, too."

"Save it for how long? A couple weeks? We're failing, Hannah. The curse is winning."

"We'll see about that. It's not over yet."

She hung up the phone and powered it down. Waverly could wait—she was the last person Hannah felt like talking to. Instead, she went downstairs to convince her dad to lose another pile of paperwork.

The next day, Hannah felt as if she had a big red target on her back, and it didn't help that she was wearing her scarlet game-day soccer uniform.

In the cafeteria, she felt eyes on her and made the mistake of glancing at Waverly. Hannah steeled herself against the beseeching look her best friend sent her. Waverly looked worse than sorry. She looked miserable. *Serves her right,* thought Hannah, slamming her lunch bag on the table next to Martin.

"I still can't believe Waverly is on their side," she said.

Martin sighed. "I don't know if that's what she meant to do. I saw Libby at Junior JET last night, and she seemed to think we were all working on the same project together. Did Waverly know what we were really trying to do? What did you tell her?"

"Not much," Hannah said. Not enough, she realized. Maybe Waverly wouldn't have believed in a tree that could text, but Hannah hadn't even told her that they were trying to save the tree itself. For all Waverly knew, they were just trying to save the messages on it—the history project. She'd been teasing Hannah about a surprise because she actually thought Hannah would be thrilled about it. "Oh, Martin, is there anything else I can mess up?"

"Hey, you're supposed to be the confident one. And we have a lot of names to research tonight—all those carvings from the tree." Martin turned his dark brown eyes to her, and she felt a little better. He was on her side.

"Did your aunt know anything about Six Sigma?" she asked.

He nodded and summarized what Michelle had said— that it was some dumb business thing that hadn't been enough to save the Happy Elf Bakery. As if anything could have beaten a curse. "I almost thought Aunt Michelle had something to do with it," Martin said, "but she thought the whole idea was stupid. Should we go to my house or yours after school?"

"Neither," she said, gesturing to her clothes. "I have a game today. But you could come over for dinner…"

"Okay," Martin said, answering before she got the words out.

"My dad will pick you up—we get pizza on the way home. What do you like on yours?"

"Everything. Anything. Nothing. Whatever."

Way to narrow things down, Hannah thought. No wonder they had so much trouble identifying suspects. They'd eliminated Jenna, but the rest of the town? The so-called bad one could be anybody.

Hannah saw her dad's big red sweatshirt as soon as she trotted onto the field. She signaled with her whole arm, and he waved back from the green folding chair amid the other parents on the sidelines. Usually Hannah's father didn't make it to her soccer games until the second half. Hannah didn't mind. He had to work until five and her games started early. Nick's and A.J.'s had always been easier to fit in, since football games took place at night or on weekends. They were true spectator sports, while nobody but relatives attended middle school girls' soccer games.

She felt an extra charge from her father's presence—she couldn't miss today, at least on the field. She scored two goals and assisted another. She flashed her dad a big grin each time, and he pumped his fist and high-fived another dad.

After the game, Hannah ran up to him and he folded her in a hug before she rolled away, leaving his arm around her shoulders.

"Dad, can we pick up Martin before we get the pizza?" she asked.

"Martin? Don't you want to go out with your teammates?" he said, frowning.

She shook her head. "It's Monday, and we have work to do on the Spirit Tree project."

"Right. The tree." Last night her dad had seemed enthusiastic and outraged when she updated him and asked for his help with Jenna's land, but this time he said it with slight distaste. They didn't speak again until she climbed into the passenger seat of their old mint-green minivan.

"We can pick up your friend," he said, clicking his seatbelt, "but we'll hold off on buying pizza."

"Okay," she said, puzzled. "Did you see the paperwork for the new parking lot they're trying to put on Jenna's land?"

"I saw it." He started the car, but didn't shift into gear. He put both hands on the wheel and looked straight ahead as other cars backed up and pulled out of the lot. "Honey, I got hold of the file, and that's the problem. My boss saw it on my desk and wondered why I had it without his permission. Then he asked what happened with Jake Laughlin's bid for the Spirit Tree removal, and I got a really bad feeling. Hannah, somebody important must have complained about the delay. My boss figured out it's my fault."

Hannah's father turned to her and spoke slowly. "He suspended me without pay. My job at the Lower Brynwood Planning Commission is hanging by a thread, pending review. I'm about to be fired."

Hannah had caused it. He didn't say it, but he didn't need to. She was trying to beat this curse, and it was fighting back. "I'm sorry, Dad," she said. "Forget the pizza. Forget everything. But I've got to talk to Martin. Could you drop me off at his house?"

When Martin opened the fiberglass door, his eyes were puffy and red-rimmed. Then he noticed the green van pulling away behind her. "What about dinner?"

"Pizza's off. It's bad, Martin. The curse is hurting people—even killing them. And now it's after our parents."

"How did you know?" he said, his voice creaky. He had been crying, and Hannah felt cold.

"Know what?"

"My mom. She's hurt—took a half-dozen pieces of shrapnel in an Afghan convoy explosion."

"Oh my God, Martin," she said, putting out her hand to touch him. He backed away and wouldn't look at her.

"She says she's going to be all right. She's says they're just scratches," he said. "And she's not coming home—the Army's going to patch her up, slap some Band-Aids on her arms and legs, and send her back out there so some other Taliban creep can take another shot at her."

"It's not your fault, Martin."

"Not my fault? Of course not. She's out there every day, seven thousand miles away in Afghanistan. She's trying to help people, but there are people who want to kill her. That's what's real. I can't keep her safe. I can't do anything to help her at all. I thought if we lifted the curse I could protect her. How stupid. I'm just some little kid who believes in spells and curses. Like Santa Claus is going to grant my wish and save my mommy for me. But the truth is, I can't save even one rotten old tree."

"We can do it, Martin. You know we have to." The pain on his face was so intense that Hannah could feel it radiating from him like heat from a fire, but he still wouldn't look at her. She wished she could comfort him, but she didn't know how.

"No, now I know I'm delusional. I'm done with the Spirit Tree, Hannah. The curse can take this whole city down, as long as it leaves me and my mom alone," he said, stumbling on the threshold as he backed inside. He shut the door on her.

She stood for a moment, wondering if she should knock again. Instead, she started the long walk home—slow this time. She didn't much care when she got there.

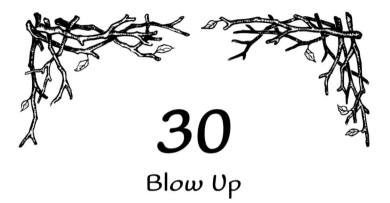

30

Blow Up

Going slow helped Hannah see more clearly. She noticed the dented trashcans behind cracked vinyl fences, the peeling paint on the green cast-iron street signs, the plastic flowers stuck in window boxes because real flowers wouldn't grow. She couldn't fix that stuff. She'd made a mistake asking her dad to compromise his job, and she couldn't fix that. But she wasn't giving up on the Spirit Tree.

She walked along the edge of Brynwood Park. The shortest way home was straight through it, but she didn't want the shortest way today. She didn't want to face the tree alone. That sounded stupid even in her head, but night fell earlier than just a few weeks ago, and the woods were darker than the street. Her mom had always warned her not to cut through them after nightfall—supposedly that's where the delinquents smoked, drank, or did mysterious bad things. She had scoffed at the idea of bad things happening in such a pokey little forest, but what could be worse than cursing a town?

What really scared her were the trees themselves. Could they sense her, like the Spirit Tree did? Were they like drones, like the hemlock outside her window, serving the tree itself?

Did all trees have their own wills—their own motives? She didn't want to find out.

She sniffed, and caught a whiff of caramel that set her mouth watering. Was she imagining it? Another breath and she smelled an acrid undertone, like a s'more too burnt to eat. When Hannah stepped clear of the treeline she saw smoke, a lot of it, choking and thick, coiling like a black snake from the town center. A distant fire siren blared, then a closer one, and Hannah walked faster. She thought of Martin's mom, caught in an explosion in a war zone. Was this what life was like for her? Like the world could burn down or implode at any minute? Hannah felt like the earth could collapse under her feet, or she could be sucked into oblivion by some giant, swirling vortex at any moment.

She was relieved to see the light of the TV flickering through the window when she finally got home. Hannah's father muted the sound.

"I was worried—I tried to reach you," he said.

She pulled her phone out of her pocket. Finally she had airtime, but she had never turned the phone on. She hadn't wanted anyone to reach her. "Sorry."

"The point of that gizmo isn't so you can text Waverly all day," he said. Hannah cringed, because he was so wrong about what she had been doing. "It's so I know you're safe."

"I'm sorry. I'm sorry about everything," she said, her voice sticking in her throat.

"Look, Hannah, what happened with my job isn't your responsibility. I'm a grown man. I make my own decisions. One of them is to be proud of you. You played great today on the soccer field, but what you're trying to do with the community history project…that's bigger than the game. It's real."

She gave a half-smile, her shoulders still hunched, and glanced at the TV behind her dad. The screen churned with smoke, flame, and plumes of water evaporating into spray.

She could still smell smoke in her nostrils, as if the fire were in the room with them.

"What's going on?" she said. "I heard the sirens."

Her dad shrugged. "The Happy Elf Bakery is burning down—five alarms. The blaze started hours ago, but they can't stop it. Looks like the place got hit by a bomb—all that old sugar and flour is pretty flammable, I guess."

"Oh, no. That's awful."

"No great loss. Some of the guys in the city planning office hoped they could bring another manufacturer in. Some of them thought we'd attract a developer to turn it into lofts, get some hip young people to live downtown. I knew none of that would ever happen in Lower Brynwood. Might as well burn it down."

Hannah had never heard her father sound so negative. Is that what the curse did? Destroy businesses, buildings, opportunities, lives, hope? What was happening to this town? To her family? Hannah's father looked at her, brightening slightly, as if he'd forgotten she was there for a moment.

"There's pizza in the kitchen," he said. "Just the cheapie frozen kind tonight, but it's not bad. Grab a few slices, kiddo, and don't forget to drink your milk."

Hannah balanced her dinner next to the kitchen computer, plugged in her phone charger, and pulled out the Spirit Tree notebook.

She'd always thought that being decisive was the right way to operate—choose, then commit right away. Don't overthink things, since first instincts were usually right. That worked on the soccer field, but this wasn't a game. This was real life.

She shook her head. She had started out wanting to save the tree and hopefully help her brother win some football games. But now the fate of the whole town rested on her, even if no one knew it. She couldn't eliminate any clues or suspects yet—not even Jenna. What did they really know about her motives? And maybe they shouldn't cross off Jake yet, but there were other people she and Martin hadn't even considered. Hannah started cross-referencing any recognizable names with the two yearbooks.

Margie Riley is EZ. Margie, a freshman in 1989, stared out at her from page sixty-seven, looking startled beneath a stand of hair so big it could have been electrified. Poor Margie. Hannah looked her up on Facebook. So, good old Margie had gotten married at some point—three kids and a husband, living out in Montana, where probably no one knew she used to be EZ.

Margie Riley didn't look like someone who would curse a tree, but then, what would that look like? Probably not like foxy Mark Caputo, who wasn't in the yearbook but was on Facebook, or Diane Papapian and Mike Foley, who had been voted cutest couple in 1990 but didn't seem to exist in the digital world.

She launched the computer's clunky old photo program and scrolled through the digital photos—there were hundreds of them. She'd snapped away, circling the trunk, capturing images of every inch of bark from the roots up. Hannah noticed that one carving practically circled the whole trunk, the letters wide and flattened, so big that it had been intersected by other carvings. Hannah clicked on the thumbnail, and the photo sharpened. *To Brynwood 1997*, she read silently. Well, whoop-dee-doo. To Brynwood. To life.

Then she squinted. The other carvings seemed to have been made over the top of this one, but how was that possible? One of them said 1990 and one was 1994. Older carvings should have been *under* the 1997 carving, not on top. So, *To Brynwood 1997* had been written first, but how?

Hannah zoomed in close. Her eyes widened. She had read the letters wrong—a flat hatch mark wasn't part of the bark's texture, but an additional letter that had nearly faded with time. She had read the date wrong, too—she had expected it to read 1997, but that wasn't what the carving really said.

Tho. Brynwood 1797.

1797. With a shock she recognized the name and date— Thomas Brynwood, who had founded the town after the Revolutionary War. Could the carving really be that old?

Hannah flipped through the yearbook to find the business card Jenna had given her. She attached the digital file to an email.

Dr. Blitzer, please take a look. You said you thought the tree was over 250 years old. The park used to be the site of the old mill during and after the Revolutionary War. Do you think this arborglyph was really made by Thomas Brynwood?

Hannah hit send, but felt like kicking herself. If she had misread that carving, what else had she missed? She pulled up the photo of the six sigmas and zoomed in, one hundred fifty percent, then two hundred percent, then four hundred percent. There, in the third row of Greek letters, running into another carving that read *Saligia rules,* she could now make out another faded letter.

There were seven characters on the tree, not six.

Seven sigmas. Time to Google.

Only one exact match—Wikipedia.

SEVEN SIGMA IS A SHORTHAND EXPRESSION FOR "THE SEVEN HABITS OF HIGHLY SUCCESSFUL EXECUTIVES," A SELF-HELP METHODOLOGY THAT EMERGED IN THE 1980s AND 1990s.

THIS ARTICLE IS A STUB. YOU CAN HELP WIKIPEDIA BY EXPANDING IT.

Well, gosh, thanks, she thought. *If I find anything more, I'll be sure to let Wikipedia know. In the meantime, if there are Seven Habits of Highly Successful Executives, I'd sure as heck like to know what they are.*

Her phone rang. Waverly.

She sighed. She didn't have time to patch up her oldest friendship tonight. But the longer she waited, the worse she felt. And Hannah figured a highly successful executive would take the call, so that's what she did.

Waverly's familiar voice rushed at her. "I didn't mean to hurt you, Hannah. Honest—Libby told me you'd like it. She said we'd be working on the same project. I'm sorry if I took all the glory."

"Is that what you think I'm mad about?" Hannah asked. "You taking the credit?"

"What else?"

"Waverly, didn't you realize that Martin and I are trying to save the tree? And you're trying to destroy it?"

No answer, and Hannah could hear tinny music in the background, as if she were on hold. Then Waverly said, "Noooo. I'm trying to preserve it—like you. Coach Laughlin told us the tree's good as dead. If we polyurethane all the messages, they'll live on for posterity. And we're building a stadium for the town. Just think—when we're in high school, you'll play soccer there."

Hannah didn't know what to say. Waverly really had been trying to help. She'd never told her best friend what she was really doing. She hadn't trusted her enough. Hannah was to blame, not Waverly.

She took a deep breath. "Listen for a sec. I know you don't understand why I'm mad, but it's okay. I'm not mad anymore. I should have told you how I felt from the beginning."

"Well, duh. But you've been spending all your time with Mar-tin," she said, pronouncing all the letters in his name in a singsong, as if she was about to launch a verse of "Hannah and Martin Sitting in a Tree."

"It's not like that. We're just partners on the project. Or we were," Hannah said, wondering if she was telling the truth. She didn't know how she felt about Martin anymore.

Or how she felt about anything. "I'll explain everything soon."

"Are you coming to my house tomorrow before school? When you didn't show up this morning, I think my dad missed you more than he'd miss me. I didn't tell him we were fighting because I knew he'd take your side."

Good old Dr. Wiggins. "I'll be there."

So, the Spirit Tree was doomed, her dad was jobless, Jenna was about to lose her land, the Happy Elf Bakery was toast, Martin's mom, Nick, even Coach Schmidt were hurt. She didn't even want to think about Mr. Richardson and Mrs. Quillen. At least she had smoothed things over with Waverly.

Nick came into the room, his hair wet from the shower.

"Hey, I heard you had a good game," he said.

"You should've seen it," she answered. He grabbed a carton of orange juice from the fridge and stood behind her chair. She turned to look at him. "I guess you *would* have seen it, if you wanted to. Didn't have practice today, did you?"

He gulped from the carton, then shook his head. "Coach Laughlin said I can resume drills Wednesday. I was too busy moping around here to realize I should have been there, Hannah. You never miss my games—I probably owe you about a hundred by now."

"More than that."

"I never thought it mattered as much to you."

"Why? Because I'm a girl?" Hannah crossed her arms in front of her.

"No, 'cause you're good at everything you do. You're the family superstar, even if you don't know it. Face facts. I'm not getting into any decent school unless it's because of football. But you could do anything, Banana."

"You could, too. You can go to college if you really want to. You and A.J. both."

He turned his back and put the carton away. "Now you sound like Coach and his Seven Habits of Highly Successful Executives again."

"What?"

"Yeah. Something about how the answer to all your problems is that you just need to ask for what you want, and the universe supplies it. You want it enough, you've got it. Some garbage like that. At this point, the universe owes me even more than *I* owe you."

Ha. The universe owed Hannah some answers. And she was hoping Jake would be the one to supply them. He might not be the leader of whatever crazy mojo cursed the Spirit Tree, but he probably knew who was.

31

The Spirit Tree

The greed of the bad one would never be satisfied. The stolen life that surged through the tree was tainted now by death and destruction. The tree could feel the incessant suck and drain through its branches and roots. The bad one wouldn't stop until the tree was dead, poisoned by despair, crumbled into dust for the bad one to consume.

The boy and girl had come again. The tree sensed their comfort and anger as energy the bad one couldn't steal, a small core of light and heat the vampire couldn't touch. It felt their light and heat even now, brightness through the fog of despair, pure energy carried as waves on the wind, anger and compassion vibrating through the earth, life force transmitted by roots that crisscrossed and tangled beneath the ground.

The tree felt closer to death, yet stronger than it had since the day the bad one's blade scarred its bark.

It hoped it was strong enough.

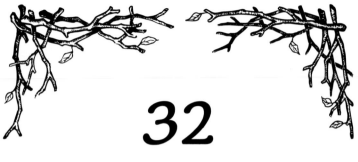

32

Seven Habits of Highly Successful Executives

Martin watched Hannah stroll into social studies with Waverly, their heads bent together as if nothing had happened. As if Waverly weren't in league with their worst enemy. As if Martin no longer existed.

Martin wished he had his iPod to protect himself from being alone. Well, from *looking* alone. But Hannah knew that it was broken and always had been. She'd probably laughed over it with Waverly. She'd gone to their side, where she belonged.

Last night, after he had talked to his mom, the only other person he'd wanted was Hannah. When she showed up on his doorstep, he'd driven her away. Just as well.

It had been a mistake to get involved here in Lower Brynwood, tree or no. Wild sylvans, dryads, serewoods—none of them could be trusted. Why would the Spirit Tree be any different? Why would Hannah? She was the real sorceress, but he had been wrong about one thing. They weren't a team. Real life was like a multiplayer RPG, after all—even in a guild, everyone was in it for themselves.

His mom had seemed all right when they'd video chatted the night before, but Martin didn't feel any better. Just because she looked and sounded fine didn't mean she was. Crap, he probably looked and sounded fine, but he was lying. He wasn't fine. He was alone here. And seeing his mom over a video screen wasn't enough.

He wanted her to tousle his hair and straighten his shirt collar before school. He wanted her to grill the steaks while he made the salad on Sunday night. He wanted to run next to her, to show her how fast and strong he was, to hear her heavy breath and know she was really alive, not pixels bouncing off a satellite somewhere. Not just a video avatar, like some character in *Dragon Era*.

He could tell Hannah was trying to get his attention, but he just stared at his hand as he drew a ranger in battle to rescue a sorceress from the Arlithean and Worlinzer mercenaries. The hordes were vaguely grotesque, but this time Martin made sure the sorceress looked like his mother—small and strong, short dark hair cut to her jawline, kind eyes that were looking at something else, as if she didn't want to be rescued and didn't even know that he was trying.

Mr. Michaelson stood in front of the class, cleaning his glasses. Martin turned his notebook to a blank page.

He didn't glance at Hannah again until two periods later, when he slumped over his cafeteria tray. He would have ignored her then, too, but she ducked her head into the space between him and his food, giving him no choice but to look at her.

"Martin," she said, turning her earring, brownish-gray eyes wide, "I need to talk to you."

"What? What do you have to say? Are you breaking up the project?"

"Are you kidding? No," she said, straightening up and taking a seat next to him. Their shoulders nearly touched, and when he saw her freckles up close he became conscious of the blackheads in the corners of his own nose. He backed away. "I found out something else. So much. We have to interview Jake. We've got early dismissal today, so we should be able to catch him before football practice. Come with me."

"You're not still stuck on that guy, Hannah, are you? You pretend to be so logical, Sherlock Holmes Barbie, but you're just guessing. And you're usually wrong." Some other kids were staring at him now. He had been shouting without meaning to.

Hannah's smile had wiped away. Then she said in a whisper that was louder than yelling, "Well, I deserve anything bad you can say to me. But you can't just walk out now."

"You're the one who walked off! You're the one who's back with Waverly."

"Only because I listened to you!" Hannah was really yelling now. "It's your turn to listen. You can't go backward, Martin. Not after everything that's happened to all of us. If you're just waiting for the year to end and everything to go back to normal, you're out of luck. There's no such thing as normal! There's just the way things are."

He shook his head. "I don't care about normal. I don't care about the tree, or Lower Deadwood. This isn't my town. I was doing this for *her*," he said, his voice breaking at the end. He couldn't bear to say "Mom" aloud.

Hannah's eyes, blazing a minute earlier, softened. Her hand twitched, and he thought for a moment she was going to reach out to him, and all his anger ran out. He wanted her to understand. "I wanted to protect her," he began, faltering. "I wanted to save her from a curse, from everything. What a dope I am. I can't even protect a tree."

"Look, I wanted to break the curse so that Nick would win a stupid football game," Hannah said, as if it embarrassed her now. "At least you had a decent reason for getting involved. And maybe it even worked. Your mom got hurt, but she's going to be okay. She's going to come home and take you away from this and you'll never have to see us again—not the tree, Lower Brynwood, Jake, or me."

He listened, and he didn't know what to feel. He missed his mom so much it hurt, but Hannah mattered, too, whether he wanted her to or not.

"Before you go, we have to save the tree," she said. "Not because it's going to do anything magic for us, but because we *should*. We can do it, Martin. The Spirit Tree wouldn't have called us otherwise."

"It called us because we were there," he grumbled.

"So what? We were there because we were the right ones." Her voice got quiet again with those last words. Martin's face had never felt hotter, but he wasn't angry. He wasn't even embarrassed, even though he knew half the cafeteria was eavesdropping. Most of these people had never noticed him before this moment—he didn't care what they thought of him. But he did care about Hannah.

She glanced around, noticing for the first time that everyone was watching. Then she leaned in so that no one else could hear. "I know I don't know everything, Martin. I need your help. Last night I found a seventh sigma in the carving, and do you know what that stands for? The Seven Habits of Highly Successful Executives."

Martin jumped.

Hannah continued, "And do you know who talks about that all the time?"

"Junior Junior Executives of Tomorrow!" Martin said. Everything clicked into place. He had known it from the very first meeting—there was no way that weird motivational crap was anything but evil.

Hannah gasped. "No! Jake Laughlin. Are you saying Junior JET talks about it, too?"

"Practically nothing else. Holy crap, I knew they were creepy all along."

"And I knew Jake was involved with the tree, even if he's not in charge. This is bigger than him. He's just a tool. Martin, you have to come with me to interview him. The curse is getting stronger. Look at this."

She pulled out A.J.'s map of Lower Brynwood. "See these Xs? These are trees dying all over town. There are broken sewers and power lines everywhere, too. And look!" She pointed out the site where the Happy Elf Bakery had stood before the fire. "The curse destroyed the factory. Gone, off the face of the earth. Brynwood Park Mall is sinking into the pit left behind. Anything in town could be next, not just the Spirit Tree."

She took his hand, more like she was shaking it in agreement than she was holding it, her fingers warm on his. He glanced around. The cafeteria had nearly emptied while they were talking. Everybody was out in the sunny courtyard now, and the bell would ring any minute for the end of lunch. He didn't want it to.

"Come with me after school," Hannah said. "Just one more period to sit through after lunch, then we have work to do."

He stared at the map of Xs, not answering, but he shook her hand slightly. He knew he'd follow her. He'd probably follow her off a cliff if she asked.

To change the subject, he asked, "So, what do those circles mean?"

"What circles?"

"The different-colored Xs form concentric circles. Look." He picked up a pencil and connected the Xs, drawing a circle through the black Xs, then concentric circles through the blue, red, and gray. The center of the circles was the Spirit Tree—the eye of the storm.

Hannah's eyes widened. "A.J. used a different color pen to mark the downed trees each day. It's a pattern. Whoever the bad one is, this curse is killing more and more things.

The Happy Elf factory is on the inner ring, the first dead zone. And here's the football field, where Coach Schmidt got sick. With the trees dead, the bad one has to destroy more and more. Causing bad luck isn't enough. Causing pain isn't enough. It needs more fuel. Look." She pointed to a blue X on the map.

"What is it?" Martin said.

"That's where my mom works—right next to the factory. Brynwood Park Continuing Care. Mom's patients have been fading, even dying, and it's right near the center of the map. They're the weakest people in town, and something is draining the life out of them. Anybody there could be next, unless we save them."

Martin felt himself growing angry again. He didn't try to squelch the feeling. What was happening was wrong. His mom never needed his help—she was strong, and so was he. Lower Brynwood had so little life left, just like those people in the nursing home. Who was so greedy that they would steal the last crumbs of life from a starving person? The bad one was a monster, whoever it was.

Martin's anger hardened into steel. "Even if nobody in Lower Brynwood knows it, we're going to save them all. Starting with the Spirit Tree."

The bell rang, but he was ready for it.

Hannah hefted her bag across her body when she saw Martin waiting at the south exit, closest to the high school in the Lower Brynwood municipal complex. It was a cruddy collection of rinky-dink buildings.

"My dad works in there," Hannah said. "Or used to. He always said the fate of the town depends on what happens there. Hard to believe."

"Harder to believe it depends on us," said Martin, half a smile crooking one corner of his mouth.

Hannah heaved a big sigh, then a smaller one. After a moment she gave Martin a sideways smile and nudged him, shoulder to shoulder.

"Race you to the high-school gym?" she said. "Just watch your step in the recycling center. I've heard there are rats as big as pit bulls."

"Let's walk, then," Martin answered, grinning. "Conserve energy in case the rats come after us."

Martin wasn't used to walking, and the pace made talking easier—almost obligatory. Too bad his tongue was still tied in knots around Hannah.

"How do you know Jake will see us?" Martin asked after a moment. They skirted along a razor wire-topped fence protecting empty garages that smelled like they housed trash trucks, a fragrant blend of hot garbage and exhaust fumes. What was the point of razor wire? Who'd want to break in there? Maybe the rats needed to be shielded from burglars.

"We'll walk into his office in the Lower Brynwood athletic department, whether he invites us or not," Hannah said. "A.J. says he knocks off work early, using the time to map his masterful football offense. Or something. And Nick told me where to find him."

"Just because we track him down doesn't mean he'll tell us anything," Martin said, although he doubted anyone could resist Hannah.

"He will. He barely recognizes my face, but I've known him for seven years. He likes to talk. He loves himself. He's riding high on the stadium and the coaching job—he won't be able to shut up."

"So, how do we get into the high school?" he asked as they approached the sprawling brick and steel building.

It had an odd, gap-toothed look from the variety of mismatched replacement windows.

"High school's in session, and security won't let us in without a good reason. The doors are all locked, but you can still open them from the inside—fire codes. Nick says that the door nearest the gym is where kids escape when cutting last period. It has the worst security camera coverage. Someone will come out sooner or later, and that's how we get in."

They stood, shifting from foot to foot like street-corner criminals. After five minutes, two girls fell through the door, stifling giggles. They shut up when they saw two people lurking in the alley, but laughed harder when they realized it was two middle-schoolers. Hannah stuck her foot in the open door.

"The athletic offices are this way," she said, gesturing with a toss of her ponytail.

"Are you sure?

"Nick and A.J. both play basketball, too—I've been coming here since I was five."

Jake was in his office, dressed in the same sharp suit he'd had on at the game, studying a desk full of diagrams. He looked up when they knocked, but didn't seem to recognize them.

"Coach Laughlin?" Hannah said. "It's Hannah Vaughan, Nick and A.J.'s sister."

He lit up. "The Spirit Tree girl," he said. "Props for steering me toward that fund-raising idea. That was money, literally. Take a load off."

"Thanks. Coach, you remember my friend, Martin," she said as if he did, but Jake showed zero sign of familiarity as he sized Martin up. Hannah sat down, her back straight, and nudged a chair toward Martin with her toe. The chair screeched, but he wouldn't sit. "He's my partner on the project."

"I thought you were working with those two cute little girls who are selling the tree."

Martin sniffed. "Waverly and Libby? No way."

Hannah craned her head around to glare at him, then turned back to Jake. "We're doing the history side of the project—how the carving of the Spirit Tree started, what the messages mean. Could we ask you a few questions? We've found your name written there a couple times."

He chuckled. "Yeah, I plan to get those sections lacquered for myself. They'll look great in my office."

Trophies hung on his wall like the head of a dead lion— Martin felt like screaming.

"That would be some kind of statement," Hannah said. "But I'm wondering if you remember when they were carved."

"Sure, I remember. I was a senior, coming off my junior champion season—the best year of my life. I didn't know it was going to end. The Spirit Club thought of carving the tree to celebrate the first football game. To pump us up," he said, looking thoughtful. A light went on behind his eyes. "You know, I didn't even realize it until now, but the person who started the carving was the same person who got me involved with the Brynwood Estates Community Association."

Hannah threw an elbow behind her and got Martin in the ribs, and he realized his mouth was hanging open. He shut it.

"Funny, I forgot she was involved—she was kind of a nerd," said Jake. "I didn't notice the Spirit Club or business geeks back then. No offense—I was kind of cocky in the old days. Had a run of bad breaks. Never thought at my age I'd still be cutting stinking lawns the way I did when I was twelve years old, but there I was. But since I joined the association, that's all over. Two months ago she approached me to join, and it's like magic. I'm halfway into the Seven

Habits of Highly Successful Executives, and all of a sudden I'm the head coach of the football team. I've won my first game, got appointed chair of the stadium fund-raising committee, and have a lock on the contract to clear Jenna's property and landscape the new stadium grounds. All thanks to one person."

"Michelle Medina," Martin said, almost whispering.

"You know her?" Jake said, surprised.

"She's my aunt, remember?"

"Oh, yeah, right. You're a lucky boy. You follow Michelle Medina, before long you'll be ruling the world with the rest of us."

"The rest of you?"

"Brynwood Estates Community Association and Junior Executives of Tomorrow. Your friend Libby will tell you all about it. If you don't get what you want when you ask for it, you demand it. The universe answers."

This wasn't the answer Martin wanted. But he realized he had known it all along. Aunt Michelle was behind everything.

33

Saligia Rules

Hannah and Martin left so quickly Jake was probably still bragging while they were halfway down the hall. Everyone knew Michelle Medina thought that she was the center of power in Lower Brynwood. It was a joke—she was the Dr. Evil of the Brynwood Estates Community Association. But it turned out she wasn't having delusions of grandeur. Jake looked like a fool, too, with all of that nonsense he'd been spouting to A.J. The joke was the perfect cover, although Hannah doubted he did it on purpose.

Martin looked dazed when they stepped into the sunlight. High-school kids streamed from all exits, hopping into beaters, muscle cars, and late-model SUVs, backing up, peeling away. Hannah said Martin's name. He watched the cars as if seeing a pattern, elaborate choreography amid the near-miss fender-benders.

"Martin," she said, grabbing his arm, glee rising in her throat. "The bad one is Michelle. We've got her now."

He shook his head. "We don't. I've been living in her... her lair, and I didn't see a thing. And how are we going to 'get' her? How do we break a curse? All we know is that she's the one who started the tree carvings."

"That's not all we know. We know she started the Spirit Tree ceremony, and that's when everything went wrong. We know she's been ruling over this town through the Community Association, and that's how she brought Jake into her plan."

"And Libby," Martin said, grudgingly. "The Junior Junior Executives of Tomorrow are all part of it—I would have noticed if I had been paying the least bit of attention."

"Well, who could? If those meetings were filled with the kind of stuff Jake says, I'd tune them out, too. The Spirit Tree is the key to her power—or at least it was. Something's changing, or Michelle wouldn't be making Jake cut the tree down for her. If we can figure out what's changed, we can stop Michelle, and we can save the tree."

"And this whole miserable town," Martin said.

"It's miserable because of her," Hannah said sharply. "But we have two advantages."

"Our numbers? Our power?" he said with one eyebrow raised. "Our tremendous pull on the Lower Brynwood City Council, now that Aunt Michelle got your dad fired?"

"Just suspended," Hannah said, frowning. "Seriously. Advantage one, Michelle doesn't know we're trying to stop her. If what Jake, Waverly, and Libby say is true, she thinks we're on her side, more or less."

"What else?"

"Two, we have an inside man." Hannah put her finger in the center of Martin's chest and tapped it. He looked at her finger and she drew it away, pretending to straighten her ponytail. "We have access to her lair, as you called it."

Hannah had never felt so nervous; standing on the step of Michelle's house gave her the willies. Martin held his breath, too—impressive after the sprint from the high school—as he turned the key.

"Aunt Michelle?" he called. No answer. "Excellent. Into the lair." He held the door for Hannah and she ducked in, brushing his arm.

"Where do we start?" Hannah asked.

"I'm not digging in her underwear drawer," said Martin, shuddering.

"How about the office? We're allowed to use the computer, so if she catches us, we have an excuse for being there." Hannah thought about her words—*if she catches us*. What would Michelle do? How much power did she have? She was evil enough to curse a whole town. To drain it, even kill. What would she do to two kids who stood in her way?

Martin booted up the computer as cover, and Hannah noticed a set of Lower Brynwood yearbooks, 1987 through 1990. How had they missed them? She browsed the Lucite awards lining the shelves, looking for any other clues they hadn't noticed. Employee of the Year from Horizon Network Communications, Businesswoman of the Year from the Lower Brynwood Chamber of Commerce, random tokens of appreciation from the Kiwanis, the Lions, the Garden Club, the Lower Brynwood Athletic Boosters. Michelle must have spent half her life at awards banquets in her own honor. Like a deity collecting offerings.

Right in the middle was a small brass plaque. Hannah picked it up to take a closer look.

"Hey!" said Martin. "We got an email from Jenna. It's marked urgent."

"No way! Maybe she's gotten the Spirit Tree declared a national Champion Tree. Jake won't be able to cut it down."

"'*Good news, bad news,*'" Martin read aloud.

"Let me read, too," Hannah said, leaning in behind him, the award gripped in her hands. "The good news had better outweigh the bad."

First the bad news. While the dimensions of the Spirit Tree are impressive, the Arbor Society reports that another American beech near Pittsburgh, while narrower in trunk girth, is nearly ten feet taller and thus retains status as Champion Tree.

But the good news is very good. Hannah, I sent the photo of the arborglyph to a colleague in the anthropology department, and he wants to study it further. He believes that this may be a genuine carving in the hand of Thomas Brynwood dating back to 1797. If so, the Spirit Tree can be protected as a Witness Tree and a historical landmark. Whether or not the arborglyph is genuine, he has filed a temporary restraining order against the tree's removal until the historical investigation can be completed.

Hannah whooped. "We won, Martin! They won't be able to cut the tree down now."

"That's only part of what we need to do," Martin said. "That gives us time to lift the curse, but we still don't know how."

Hannah felt the weight of the brass award in her hands and studied it. Engraved on the center:

$$7\Sigma$$

Hannah peered at the smaller letters written beneath it: THE SALIGIA RULES.

"*Saligia rules!*" she said. "That was carved on the tree."

"What?" Martin said. "Who's Saligia?"

"I don't know." Hannah grabbed her bag, spilling papers as she pulled the notebook out. She found the photo of the seven sigmas—she'd stared at those letters so often that she barely thought about the carving beneath it. "There was nobody named Saligia in any of the yearbooks that I remember. I don't think it's a person at all."

She pulled up a search window and typed in the word. She clicked on the first result.

SALIGIA IS AN ACRONYM BASED ON THE LATIN WORDS FOR THE SEVEN DEADLY SINS. SUPERBIA, AVARITIA, LUXURIA, INVIDIA, GULA, IRA, ACEDIA.

"The Seven Habits of Highly Successful Executives," said Martin. "Pride, avarice, extravagance, envy, gluttony, anger, uneasiness."

"Where does it say that?" Hannah asked, skimming the page but not finding the words.

"It doesn't. But those are the Seven Habits of Highly Successful Executives that Junior Junior Executives of Tomorrow was trying to teach us. That's what Jake was talking about when he told us how he'd gained sudden power."

"Seven Sigma is the Seven Deadly Sins?" Hannah's head spun. "What kind of cult is this?"

Aunt Michelle's voice rang out from the doorway. "Not a cult," she said, her voice lilting cheerfully. "A philosophy. Once upon a time certain leaders tried to convince common people that ambition was a bad thing. But those leaders themselves always knew the Answer." She smiled at Martin and Hannah, but the expression didn't reach her eyes.

Hannah put her hand on Martin's arm, cautioning him to stay silent. Maybe Michelle didn't know what they were trying to do. Maybe she hadn't heard much. She might still think they were on the same side. Hannah smiled back. If she had ever been persuasive in her life, now was the time.

"You mean, Seven Sigma is like the secrets of success?" Hannah leaned in toward Michelle, trying to look interested and relaxed when all she wanted to do was make a break for the door.

The corners of Michelle's eyes crinkled, and Hannah thought she believed her. "Exactly. It's the Answer. Throughout the ages, only a few have known it, but those people have ruled—Machiavelli, Borgia, Raleigh, Sun, Morgan, Oppenheimer, Rand, Milken, Madoff. And now little me in Lower Brynwood." She batted her eyes.

Hannah nudged Martin again, trying to get him to loosen his fists. She stood calmly and asked, "So, what's the Answer? How did you find it?"

"I'd like to say I owe it to Junior Executives of Tomorrow, but they owe it to me," she said, dusting an invisible speck of dust off a gaudy award. Probably to draw attention to it. Michelle turned toward them and continued, "Back in high school, they had a consultant from the Happy Elf Bakery come talk to us to tell us about how Six Sigma processes would make American manufacturing competitive. But I knew it would never go far enough to make a difference. The summer between my junior and senior year, I saw a flyer about an all-day seminar that promised to teach the Seven Habits of Highly Successful Executives. I took the train to a hotel ballroom downtown and paid my entrance fee—half the college money I had saved. Best money I ever spent. I was the only high-school kid in a room full of business suits, but I had found my calling. That's where I found it— the Seventh Sigma that failing businesses had forgotten. I learned the secret the ancient ones called the Answer."

"Like the answer to a prayer?" Hannah asked, tilting her head.

"No." Michelle shook her head and wagged her polished finger. Her voice rose. "You don't get what you want by begging for it from some daddy god. You get it by demanding it of the universe."

She's like a bully robbing the universe of its lunch money, Hannah thought. But she could tell Michelle wanted to talk. What was the good of ruling the town if you couldn't boast about it? What was it called—*Superbia*? Pride?

Hannah said evenly, "If it works so well, why doesn't everyone do it?"

"Easy. At least it's easy for me." Michelle's eyes gleamed. "Throughout history, there were always some who were afraid of power, and others who tried to keep it for themselves. The early Christian church renamed the Seven Sigma the Seven Deadly Sins and tried to eliminate them. But it turned out that when do-gooders like Thomas Aquinas defined the Seven Deadly Sins—SALIGIA—they unknowingly preserved the ancient philosophy for a select few—like me—to decode."

"I don't get it," Hannah said, shaking her head and taking a side step toward the door, as if she were just shifting her weight. She tried to catch Martin's eye, but he was glaring at Michelle. She had to keep him quiet—he looked as if he were about to explode. "If they're sins, how can Seven Sigma make you successful?"

"They're not sins—they're virtues," said Michelle, spreading her palms and fluttering her eyelashes innocently. "You've heard of the virtue of selfishness? That's just the beginning. Anger is wrath against your enemies. Envy drives you to vanquish your foes. Avarice drives you to amass more wealth. Gluttony—such an unattractive word—means that you take the resources that are yours and anything else you can get your hands on."

Martin nearly choked. "You're inhuman."

The smiling mask dropped from Michelle's face. "Wrong again, Martin," she said, a furrow appearing between her eyes like it had been cut with a knife. "Being human means gaining dominance over the natural world. And these are the principles of running a successful business."

"You call those principles?" Martin said. He edged forward, angling his shoulder in front of Hannah protectively. "You're destroying a whole town."

"This town was going down the sewer long ago, and I'm just making sure someone benefits from it—me. Martin, who has the power to change things around here? Jenna Blitzer, with her environmental fairydust? Or me, with the power of the universe behind me?" Michelle looked at him with mixed pity and disgust.

"You can twist the power for a little while, but you don't rule it, Aunt Michelle," said Martin, his voice tense with rage and his face as red as Hannah had ever seen it. Even his hair vibrated. "The Spirit Tree is alive. It has its own power. "

"Its power *is* mine, Martin. I took it and I own it," she said, a vein in her temple pulsing. "That tree has been channeling the little bit of power this town has straight to me ever since I carved the runes on it—just like the ancient practitioners of the Saligia rules. And every year, everyone who marks it has been reinforcing my hold."

"You're stealing the town's life. It's not yours." Martin shook his head.

"Power belongs to anyone with the guts to grab it." Michelle raised her chin and squared her shoulders, as if she was challenging Martin. She was taller than he was— taller than Hannah, even. "And I've been more than fair. I introduced Seven Sigma into Junior Executives of Tomorrow and the Brynwood Estates Community Association. I started Junior JET. And I've helped Jake Laughlin and everyone else who complied with me in the Brynwood Estates Community Association. If you play along, you benefit. I'm even helping you all get a new stadium—I'm the one who convinced Horizon Network Communications to fund the building."

"Why?" Martin asked, throwing back his own shoulders. "Why do you care about some dumb stadium? Why does Horizon?"

"Cell phones, of course. The new bleachers will be a giant transmission tower. Horizon gives money for construction. As Horizon vice-president, I get the credit for improving community relations. Horizon gets naming rights and a rent-free, exclusive fifty-year lease on the tower. The new signal will reach all the way to Upper Brynwood."

"Jake didn't say anything about that at the football game," Hannah said.

"Of course not," said Michelle, turning to Hannah and giving her a stiff half smile, until she saw the anger in Hannah's eyes, too. "Oh, grow up. Everyone wants a new sports stadium, but you always end up with a few nutjobs like Jenna squawking about cell phone towers interfering with bat navigation or causing brain cancer. Collateral damage. That's why Jake made the announcement for the stadium, and not the superintendent or me—to deflect attention from the connection with Horizon and the cell phones. Of course, to keep that news from slipping out, we didn't tell Jake everything."

"But what about the Spirit Tree?" Martin broke in. "Why do you have to kill it?"

"Trees were good enough at transmitting power for the ancient practitioners of the Answer, but it's time to upgrade the technology," Michelle said. "I'm too strong now—a pile of sticks can't do the job. And Lower Brynwood is dried up—I need energy from Upper Brynwood, and that's just the beginning. The tree's last job will be fueling the transfer of my power to the stadium itself."

"That's what you think," Martin said, triumph in his eyes. "You're wrong. Jenna Blitzer has the Lower Brynwood Historical Commission on the tree's side. They've declared it an historical Witness Tree. By this time tomorrow, it'll be protected by a restraining order."

Michelle's face reddened and she and Martin stared at each other, each flaring their nostrils like bulls about to charge each other. Then her eyelids flickered, as if she was thinking to herself, and she seemed to pull herself together, the line between her eyes flattening and her face becoming a mask once more. Without speaking, she left the room, clacked across the foyer, and grabbed the front-door knob with one hand while reaching into her jacket pocket with the other.

Hannah and Martin looked at each other—was Michelle retreating? Was she admitting defeat? Had they really won?

Michelle swung the door open and raised her car keys with a flourish. Then they heard the beep of a car alarm disengaging. "Who's protecting the tree right now?" she said, spitting the taunt over her shoulder, not bothering to shut the door.

Martin and Hannah stormed through it, their shoulders bumping. Michelle backed up the SUV, but Martin threw himself behind the moving car. He planted himself behind the bumper, feet wide and his facing glowing bright in the car's reverse lights. Hannah gasped when the car stuttered backwards, inches away from Martin's legs.

Michelle rolled down the window.

"I'm going for a walk in the woods," she said. "Move, Martin. Your mom's recovery might take a setback if she hears you had a tragic car accident while out running."

"She's bluffing," Hannah said, hoping it was true. Martin stepped aside.

"So was I. I don't want to get run over," he said. Michelle gave a nasty wave as she rolled out of the parking lot.

"What do we do now?" Hannah asked, nearly wailing.

"We know where she's going—to the Spirit Tree," said Martin. He seemed calm now, and when Hannah looked at him, she felt clearer, too. "But she's driving, and traffic right now is all jammed up. With all the cul-de-sacs in Brynwood Estates and all the detours from broken trees and sewers, there's no direct route."

"Unless you know the shortcuts. Do you think we can get there before her?" Hannah asked.

"We can try."

They looked at each other, and Martin smiled. *So this is what we were training for*, Hannah thought as they took off running.

34

Confrontation

The sky darkened. This wasn't just twilight—a storm came out of nowhere, clouds tumbling into existence before Martin's eyes. He and Hannah sped up, synchronized in step, breathing in time. Neither spoke—there was nothing to say, and they were going too fast, anyway.

When they reached Brynwood Park, Aunt Michelle's SUV was parked at an angle by the side of the road, headlights still on.

Hannah ducked onto the path first. The woods were dark, except where the tops of the trees caught a glint of light before the sun sank behind the ridge of houses. Martin looked up—despite the setting sun, the sky directly overhead was black. That was no ordinary cloud.

Aunt Michelle stood next to the tree, stabbing the mud with her spiky heels and brandishing something sharp in her hand. She sneered at them, and the tool in her hand buzzed to life. Martin recognized the tiny pink saw that had seemed so ridiculous in her garden tote. It didn't seem ridiculous now. He felt rage swelling in his chest. He wanted to hurt her.

"Stay away," Aunt Michelle said, waving the saw toward them. "I'm warning you now."

Martin surged forward. Hannah hauled him back toward her and spoke into his ear. "She can't possibly cut the tree down with that little saw, but she could do a lot of damage to you."

Martin nodded. Aunt Michelle would use his anger if he let her, but he was smarter than she was. He called out, "Come on, Aunt Michelle. I know you won't hurt me. You agreed to take care of me."

"More or less. I thought having a displaced Army brat living with me would help my image. Nurturing and patriotic, too—the perfect combination when I run for Congress."

"Congress?" Martin asked. He imagined Aunt Michelle in Washington—how much evil could she do with the whole Federal government at her disposal?

"Why not? I have the Seven Sigma—the Saligia rules. The ancient Answer to success—demand what you want, and the universe provides it. Do you think someone like me could be satisfied as president of a community association?"

"I don't understand," Hannah said, but Martin was sure she knew exactly what she was saying. "If you destroy the tree, doesn't your hold on the town end?"

Aunt Michelle buzzed the saw again. "The tree is a conduit—it's the transmitter that makes power flow. You know what works even better? Money. *Avaritia*. Every dollar we earn from selling off the tree transfers its power to the stadium it built. Money is power."

"You can't do that," Martin said. "If you cut down the tree now, you can't auction it off in public. The fundraiser's ruined. You're breaking the law."

"I don't need the whole tree, Martin. Enough money will flow into the stadium, with or without the fundraiser. The most important piece of the puzzle is the rune itself—the Seven Sigma. Remember the time capsule we're dedicating in the stadium with a section of the Spirit Tree? Which inscription did you think we were going to include inside?"

"That's how you were going to transfer the curse to the stadium," Martin said. The runes were going to become part of the transmission tower.

Aunt Michelle bared her teeth. "Why do you call it a curse? It's a blessing." She powered the saw again, its tiny motor thrumming, then held it above the carving that had first gotten Hannah's attention. Hannah had been right—the sigmas were the key all along.

"No!" Hannah yelled. The saw's teeth tore through living wood. Aunt Michelle chanted something over the din that Martin couldn't understand. Then he realized it wasn't English at all.

"*Superbia, avaritia, luxuria, invidia, gula, ira, acedia.*"

The wind whipped up, and Aunt Michelle's hair snaked around her face. She spoke louder. "*Superbia, avaritia, luxuria, invidia, gula, ira, acedia.*"

The saw splintered the wood as it tore through the last bit of bark.

Aunt Michelle silenced the power tool, but the wind still roared. "That's that." She held up the flayed bit of bark, peering at them through the carving as if it were a grotesque mask.

SIGMA SIGMA SIGMA SIGMA SIGMA SIGMA SIGMA. SALIGIA RULES.

"You lost, kids."

Hannah ran to the tree and placed her hand on the raw wound in the tree's side. "I'm sorry. I'm sorry."

Aunt Michelle clucked her tongue. "I know it hurts. Use that pain. If I hadn't lost the class president election, I wouldn't have joined the Spirit Club and Junior Executives of Tomorrow, and none of this would have happened. You're welcome to accompany Martin at our meetings anytime." Martin felt as if she'd slapped him when she said his name. His anger flared—he didn't know how much longer he could contain it. "Grudges are not part of the Seven Sigma. Well, some argue that grudges are a subset of wrath, but I save my wrath for those I haven't defeated. And you two are definitely losers."

"I'm never going back there," Martin said, the vow bitter but calm.

"You *are* wrathful, aren't you?" she said, throwing the saw to the ground. She dug in her giant handbag until she pulled out a Ziploc bag that still held a few rice-cake crumbs. She dumped the fragile bark in and sealed the bag with a flourish. "At least you learned something from me."

He wiped away angry tears before they could fall, then placed his hand on Hannah's, resting on the damp wood of the Spirit Tree. His fingers sparked with electricity when he touched her, his life force humming in tune with hers. He felt the strength of his anger transforming into something greater, a powerful force that flowed from his hand to hers, then into the bleeding wound in the bark.

Hannah seemed to be listening to the tree, but he couldn't hear anything. The hard core of anger loosened in his chest, and Martin spoke aloud. He didn't feel stupid. He felt strong. He knew exactly what to say. "O mighty tree, answer us."

A letter on the bark lit up, inches from Hannah's face, lighting her blonde hair in a golden halo.

The tree's answer flashed out.

THE BAD ONE FREED ME.

Martin glanced at Aunt Michelle, who was still gloating. She hadn't picked up the message, but he understood in a flash of comprehension. Aunt Michelle thought she would gain power when she cut the rune off, but she was wrong. She had unknowingly released her hold over the Spirit Tree. She couldn't use it anymore. She didn't control it.

FREE, the tree spelled again.

NOW HEAL ME.

The dark sky blazed. Hannah placed her other hand on Martin's, and he stacked his on top. Moments before, the Spirit Tree had been nearly depleted and empty. With the runes gone, it felt alive. Martin felt energy surge through him—from him, from Hannah, from the electron-charged air—and into the tree. Life rushed back into the tree, like a torrent of water once a dam has broken. It didn't hurt—it flowed through them, as natural as the blood in his veins, as soft as the warmth of the sun, but inside his nerves instead of on his skin. Martin and Hannah gave the tree its life force back.

Pure light rained from the dark clouds above, rolling into the leaves and somehow being absorbed. Each twig and root lit up, lacy and bright against the black sky and dark earth. In the glow Martin saw Aunt Michelle watching, too, her triumph gone. She looked frightened, and scrambled backwards until she stumbled and collapsed in the dirt.

The light faded. The beech's silvery bark had sealed over the gaping wound where Aunt Michelle had hacked at the tree. The only sign that she had mutilated it was a smooth spot amid the tangle of inscriptions.

"The letters!" Hannah cried. The other carvings began to glow, and she and Martin stepped back to read the message that lit up in the letters. They broke physical contact with the tree, but Martin still felt connected through the stream of energy rushing between them.

Martin read aloud as each word was completed.

SHE FREED ME.

YOU HEALED ME.

BUT TIME IS STILL UP.

"What does that mean?" Hannah wailed.

The golden fissures of light that traced the words narrowed, then sealed up. The letters disappeared, and the bark was solid, unmarked, new. The tree was really healed.

Then the whole Spirit Tree blazed again, too bright to look at. Martin shielded his eyes and pulled Hannah away, and they fell over Aunt Michelle. The three of them lay on the forest floor as the tree burned.

This was real fire, heat scorching their faces, hot ashes raining down just as light had moments before. Martin closed his eyes and hoped the others did the same. What was happening?

The fire roared, the loudest noise Martin had ever heard. Then silence, and nothing. The red behind Martin's eyelids snuffed out to black.

He opened his eyes. The tree had disappeared—the only trace was the indentation where the massive trunk had burst from the earth, a lost-wax impression of the starry knot of roots.

Martin and Hannah clutched each other, still tumbled on the ground. He looked into her stormy eyes, and she nodded. She was all right. They rolled apart.

Aunt Michelle stood, dusting off her red suit.

"Once again, sorry, kids. Time was up for the tree, I guess. It may be gone, but I have what I need," she said, recovering her smirk. She pulled the Ziploc bag from her handbag and held it in the air like a trophy. Then she noticed it was empty.

The section of carved bark was gone. Even the crumbs were gone.

"Wait," she said, rifling through her purse. She turned it upside-down, makeup and nutrition bars clattering to the ground along with the electric saw. She tossed them aside, becoming more frantic as she searched for the missing section of bark. Martin knew she wouldn't find it.

The sky lightened to twilight orange and purple, just enough sun that Martin and Hannah could watch the grass turn green where the tree had once stood. The verdant circle grew, radiating outward, spreading beneath their feet. A green curtain passed over the woods, brightening and softening the autumn gold and brown with a flush like springtime. As daylight faded, so did the green, the woods yellowing back to the golden hues of fall.

When the sky darkened to purple and the leaves and trees grayed into colorlessness, Martin smiled. They had beaten Aunt Michelle. He didn't register when she left, but he noticed when Hannah took his hand. It was warm, like the light from the tree had been. She stood, still holding his hand, and pulled him up beside her. His joints felt creaky, his muscles weak, but he didn't care. He didn't feel drained—he felt light. The energy they had given to the tree wasn't gone. It surrounded him and Hannah. They were breathing it.

They had lifted the curse. They had released the tree. The Spirit Tree was gone—every bit of it.

Martin dreamed it was daytime. He stood in a vast field, but not an empty one. All around him he listened to the buzz of birds and insects in tall stands of goldenrod, fluffy white boltonia, and wilting jewelweed, dwarfed by twelve-foot thistles.

The Spirit Tree had disappeared. Even the woods were gone, but the field was alive. And Martin was not alone.

Hannah stood beside him. She was dreaming, too.

35

Miserable Town

Things were normal in Lower Brynwood, if you could call something normal when it was the best it had ever been.

Martin and Hannah could both feel it right away. The next morning dawned the crispest, most beautiful, picture-perfect fall day they had ever seen. The leaves had turned from green to riotous bright colors overnight. Even the air tasted sweeter and cleaner.

The curse unraveled quickly. Within a few days Hannah's dad got his job back, including back pay. When his boss figured out that Jake wasn't certified for tree surgery, he suspended the town's contract with Laughlin Landscaping and Hannah's dad got credit for uncovering it.

The town lawyers turned down the planning commission's request to seize Jenna's historic property. They even chided Aunt Michelle for suggesting that Lower Brynwood could possibly benefit from destroying one of the oldest buildings in town, one with a direct connection to the town's founder, for the sake of a parking lot.

Once the controversy over eminent domain came out, Horizon Network Communications downgraded its financial support for the new stadium. The last thing they wanted was to attach their name to an unpopular project, and the deal to build a cell tower on school grounds fell through. Still, plans for a new stadium continued. The school district replaced the funds with grants, thanks to the smaller, greener stadium plan Jenna, her university colleagues, a landscape architect, and a green engineering firm had submitted months earlier, using sustainable construction materials and local labor. A.J. quit Jake's crew, got hired by the new landscape company, and re-enrolled in community college to study horticulture and ecology.

Nick even led the Lower Brynwood football team to victory over Upper Brynwood, then a few more, earning the team a winning record for the first time since the curse began.

Waverly and Libby joined forces with Hannah and Martin on their new social studies project—working with the Arbor Day Society to create a digital record of the Spirit Tree carvings using the photos Hannah and Martin had taken. It turned out Waverly and Libby were pretty good with graphics programs, thanks to their mutual obsession with the *Project Catwalk 4* video game.

But things being normal didn't mean they were perfect. It turned out Aunt Michelle was capable of holding a grudge against Martin—after all, she had nursed a one-sided rivalry with Jenna since high school. Fortunately, she had decided to tolerate his presence at home. She still needed him for her election campaign, although she scaled back her ambitions from Congress to Lower Brynwood Town Council after the debacle with the stadium.

"Great," Hannah said when Martin told her during their daily after-school run. "I think she could do more damage here. At least Washington is three hours away."

"That's what she said, but instead of damage she called it 'local impact,'" Martin said. "Aunt Michelle and I both know she changed her mind because she couldn't go to Washington without power stolen from the Spirit Tree. Now she's got to pay her dues in local politics, and I'm stuck with her, wandering around that silly house pretending the whole thing never happened."

"It shouldn't have," said Hannah, breathing a little hard. "You know, I thought if we healed the tree, it would live. I guess it really wanted us to let it go."

Letting go, Martin thought. *Not so easy.* He ran silently beside her for a half-block. He had to tell her the best news of all, the best of his life, but at that moment it didn't feel so great. When his mom had video chatted last night, he had been ecstatic, but now he realized how much he was about to lose.

"My mom is coming home, Hannah," he said at last. "Her whole unit will be back in the States by New Year's Day."

Hannah squealed and hugged him awkwardly, nearly tackling him as they broke stride. "No way! I can't believe it," she said. "Will she be able to live with Michelle, too? Talk about awkward." She laughed.

"Home is South Carolina," Martin said, then swallowed.

Hannah's laughter stopped abruptly. "You're leaving? You're not even going to finish out the school year here?"

"No." The two of them pulled onto the edge of the Brynwood Park trail. Hannah stopped, gasping hard as if she couldn't catch her breath. She leaned down, her hands braced against her knees. Martin put his hand on her back, but she threw it off.

"Well, great," she said, abrupt, as if she had slapped him. "You've been wanting to leave this…this *miserable town* ever since you got here. Lower Deadwood, right?"

"You know I don't feel that way now. Well, except for the fact that I'm still living with Aunt Michelle and she totally hates me, I like it here. I mean, I miss my mom and my friends back home, but I'm glad to be here for now."

When she looked up at him, her gray eyes brimmed with tears. She swiped them with the back of her hand and straightened. "For now? For how long? You won't even be here another three months. That's too soon to leave."

"It depends how you look at it. For the Spirit Tree, three months was nothing. But we're not trees—it's a long time for people."

"It's longer than I've known you," Hannah said. She looked away, facing the part of the woods where they had met in September. Once, this site had been the secret heart of the town, but now it was empty. The Spirit Tree was really gone.

"Three months is a long time if you make it count," Martin said. Hannah turned to him again and nodded. She peered into his eyes in that odd way she had, as if she was looking through them right into his skull.

"So, let's not waste it," she said, grabbing his hand in both of hers. He worried that his palm was sweaty, but realized that hers were, too. She helped him to his feet, and he still looked up at her slightly, close enough to count her freckles. He forgot about being nervous when she leaned down slightly to kiss him. For an instant, he felt the world stop around them. Then the buzz of life was louder than ever, ringing in his ears and through his veins.

He felt the warmth of her lips on his mouth even after she pulled away.

"Race you to the Spirit Tree," she said, turning and taking off in a sprint.

Martin was about to yell after her that the tree was already gone, but then he could see it. Shining ahead of them through the woods was a column of light a hundred and fifty feet tall, haloed by a thousand tiny branches radiating outward, forking into thousands more, each tipped in a tiny star. He held his breath for a moment.

He blinked, and the ghost image faded into his memory. For him, the tree would never really be gone. He stretched his fingers wide like the branches and felt the life flow through them. Through *him*.

He ran after Hannah.

Acknowledgements

Every book is a journey, and this one had more detours than most.

Thank you to those who helped put this book into print: editor Jennifer Carson, agent Kathleen Rushall, and cover illustrator Shawna JC Tenney.

I remain grateful for the generous writers who supported me, read drafts, and answered questions: R.M. Clark, Steven Cordero, Dee Garretson, Bryn Greenwood, Joyce Shor Johnson, Norma Johnson, Teri Kanefield, Katrina Lantz, Nikki Loftin, Colby Marshall, Tracey Martin, Michelle McLean, Jenna Nelson, Lucy Pick, Cindy Pon, Lindsay Scott, Kristal Shaff, Shveta Thakrar, Angela Townsend, and Jenn Walkup.

Thanks to all my friends in Operation Awesome, the Pit, Purgatory, and the Blueboards.

To this tally I add those who embraced this story and told others: Jenny Cross, Kate Galer, Gail McCown, Alexandra Baker Shrake, Barley VanClief, and the inimitable Todd Marrone.

Much love to those who gave me strength and time to see this through: parents Nan and Jack Andrews; sisters Kim Andrews and Heather Andrews Magda; daughters Juliette and Oona; and especially my husband Jeff.

Create happiness.

Steampunk anthology of seven short stories ranging from reimagined folk tales to unique alternate histories.

Real Girls Don't Rust

Edited by Jennifer Carson

SPENCER HILL PRESS · spencerhillpress.com

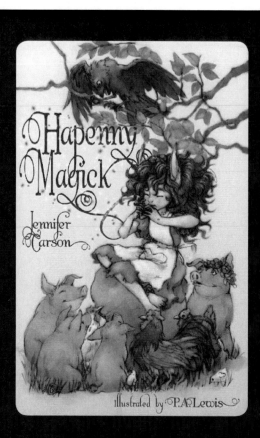

As the tiniest Hapenny, a race of little people,
Maewyn Bridgepost spends her
days from breakfast to midnight nibble
scrubbing the hearth, slopping the pigs and
cooking for her guardian, Gelbane. As if life
as a servant isn't bad enough, Maewyn learns
that Gelbane is a troll—and Hapennies
are a troll delicacy!